HOUSE VAMPIRE
THE LORENA QUINN TRILOGY

SAMANTHA SNOW

Copyright ©2017 by Samantha Snow
All rights reserved.

Get Yourself a FREE Bestselling Paranormal Romance Book!

Join the "**Simply Shifters**" Mailing list today and gain access to an exclusive **FREE** classic Paranormal Shifter Romance book by one of our bestselling authors along with many others more to come. You will also be kept up to date on the best book deals in the future on the hottest new Paranormal Romances. We are the HOME of Paranormal Romance after all!

* **Get FREE Shifter Romance Books For Your Kindle & Other Cool giveaways**

* **Discover Exclusive Deals & Discounts Before Anyone Else!**

* **Be The FIRST To Know about Hot New Releases From Your Favorite Authors**

Click The Link Below To Access Get All This Now!

SimplyShifters.com

Already subscribed?
OK, *Turn The Page!*

About This Book

The time for Lorena to decide who to choose was fast approaching.

However, with one of the original candidates deceased, Vlad decided to take matters into his own hands.

In more ways than one...

CHAPTER ONE
CHAPTER TWO
CHAPTER THREE
CHAPTER FOUR
CHAPTER FIVE
CHAPTER SIX
CHAPTER SEVEN
CHAPTER EIGHT
CHAPTER NINE
CHAPTER TEN
CHAPTER ELEVEN
CHAPTER TWELVE
CHAPTER THIRTEEN
CHAPTER FOURTEEN

CHAPTER ONE

Sometimes being a hero sucked.

Oh sure, in Hollywood they made it all explosive action sequences with dramatic music and steadily built anticipation, but that was a great big load of crap. Ninety-five percent of the time being a hero was that montage of training. It was all blood, sweat and tears drawn over a span of months. And there wasn't a whole lot of cheesy eighties music playing in the background while it happened. There was just a lot of failure, a lot of bruises, and magic blowing up in your face. Okay, that last one only happened if, like me, you were training to be a witch. That happened to me a lot, mostly because, so far as I could tell, I was the worst witch that there ever was.

It wasn't the prophecy that swam through my veins, the one that said I would give birth to the child who would bring magic back into the world. It wasn't the fact that I was a necromancer, manipulator of all the undead, it wasn't even the fact that I hadn't started learning magic until I was nineteen, not even a year ago. Heck, not even three whole months ago. Nope, I was the crappiest witch to ever sling a spell because I got the man, or rather the vampire, that I loved, killed. All because I was an idiot.

If I had known, half a year ago, that this is what would have happened when I traveled to the middle of Nowhere town in the middle of nowhere Virginia I would have just left well enough alone. I would have sucked it up and stayed at my crappy minimum wage job at the burger place with my aspirations of one day being a shift manager. It would have been much easier to ignore the stupid letter from a woman I didn't know. informing me that the grandmother I had never met, but always wondered about, was dead. Who cared if she had left me a little house and a very small fortune? Who cared if the very arrival of it marked a turning point in my life? And who really cared if it would eventually lead me to the most stoic, often grumpy, vampire and the confusing, often passionate love that would eventually blossom between us? Not me. No-siree-bob. I would have left well enough alone. I swear it.

"Lorena?"

That was my dad calling me. Ugh. My dad. The one who had carted me all over the United States, pretending that he had to take new positions inside some advertising agency so that we had never lived in a single place long enough to set down roots. To be honest, we'd never stayed anywhere long enough to set up potting soil. But oh no, that had been a great big fat lie. The truth? He'd been trying to keep me hidden from my super crazy mother. A cultist who pretty much didn't want me to fulfill my destiny as the progenitor of a new era of magic.

Right now, I was pretty pissed off at both of them for trying to make my life decisions for me. I was pissed off at Marquessa for sending me the letter. I was pissed off at me for being a failure of epic proportions. I was pretty pissed off at the world too, but it hadn't really done anything but exist.

"Lorena?" my dad called again. I continued to ignore him. I had no interest in starting up the conversation I knew he wanted to have. It was too hard to face. So was getting up, taking a shower, and other basic bodily functions. At the moment, breathing was about all I could manage, and if I was being honest I didn't even really want to do that.

Wei was dead. He was gone. Nothing in my life had ever hurt more than this.

Maahes, my tabby ghost cat, stared at me from the safe distance of a pillow. It watched me with that careful feline gaze, all bright eyes and stoic curiosity, as if it wondered what I was going to do. Him and everyone else. Everyone, for some reason, was looking to me to decide what was going to happen next. The problem? I couldn't bring myself to care enough to make a decision.

"Lorena?" he called again.

I continued to ignore him. What could he possibly want right now that was important enough to invade the nothingness that I was doing?

Maahes stretched out on top of his pillow throne. The fabric didn't respond to the motion. Why would it? Maahes was dead. Not the way that Wei was dead, Maahes was ghost dead, shuffled off his mortal toil l but still there in spirit. Nothing responded to Maahes' presence. Nothing but me. As a necromancer, I was the only thing that he could touch. His tiny paw reached out and settled on my nose. It was cold, and normally I would have moved away from it, but my body protested that.

"Lorena?"

"What!?" I finally jerked up. The motion caused the empty wrappers of what little food I'd managed to choke down these past few days to crinkle around me. I wanted to be left alone, didn't he understand that? Didn't anyone understand that? Maahes, in an act of feline dismissiveness, jumped off the pillow and hid in whatever astral realm ghosts went to when they didn't want to be seen. Then again, maybe he was just hiding under the bed. Maybe both. Probably both. Who knew what weirdness happened underneath a witch's bed? Certainly not me. I didn't know enough, not nearly enough. That was part of the problem. That thought had me flopping back down on the mattress, suddenly too exhausted to be angry.

The door to my bedroom, which had once been my grandmother's, swung open to reveal my dad. He didn't look like me, not at first. His hair was darker than my ash brown, with strands of silver sprinkled around the temples and along the top making him look artfully aged. His eyes were brown rather than my hazel. In one hand was a plate, in the other was my cell phone. I knew it was mine because of the Wonder Woman case. His brows, which I knew for a fact he brushed to make them lay flat, were drawn together with concern.

I didn't care. He could be concerned, that was his problem. You wanna know what my problem was? Death. Here I was, supposedly this prophecy ridden necromancer, master of life and death, and my almost boyfriend was dead. I was pretty sure my problem was bigger.

"You haven't eaten all day," he said.

I hadn't. I knew that. And if I was remembering right the only thing I'd managed to eat yesterday was a fruit roll-up, breakfast of champions. Eating sucked. I didn't want to do it. The idea of chewing on anything felt ridiculous and, to some extent, painful. I didn't want to eat. I wanted Wei back.

I didn't respond.

He took a few steps in. The edges of his jeans made a soft sound on the pale gray carpet. That drew my attention. My dad rarely ever wore jeans. For as long as I had known him it was all loafers and sweater vests and perfectly pressed khakis. Not like me. I loved jeans. Jeans and t-shirts and sturdy boots, that was the uniform of my life. But there my dad was, dressed more like me than himself.

Now that he was closer I could see that the plate he was holding was stacked with a club sandwich. That wasn't playing fair. Sandwiches were my all-time favorite food, and as far as I was concerned the club was the tip of the top of that group. I could smell the bacon and my mouth watered in response. Rude mouth. Didn't it know that I didn't want to eat?

"You need to eat," my dad's voice was utterly gentle. That was weird too. My dad was the kind of person who didn't suggest things, he demanded them, told them. Maybe this wasn't my dad, maybe this was some weird magic clone that was going to nice me to death. Yeah, that was logical. What was logical anymore?

"I'm not hungry."

On cue, my stomach gave a gurgle. My dad laughed. I didn't. I was thinking that my stomach was a traitor.

"Come on, I made it with swiss. Cold Dr. Pepper too."

Dang. I knew my limitations. I was willing to waste a lot of things, but not my favorite drink. I certainly wasn't about to let that go to waste. With a sigh, I sat up and held out my hand.

"Do you wanna come sit at the table?" he gave the bed a once over.

I gave him a look. I knew the bed was a mess. Hell, I was a mess. I had spent days laying in it, probably growing mushrooms out of my backside. But I wasn't getting out of bed. As far as I was concerned I lived in this bed. If he couldn't take that, then he could leave and take the sandwich with him.

After a series of meaningful looks he finally relented and handed over the plate and the tall glass filled with Dr. Pepper. I set the glass on the nightstand and the plate in my lap. For a moment, I just stared at it. It was almost like I had forgotten how to eat real food. I mean, I wasn't saying that a pack of Pringles wasn't real, but pressed and fried potato sludge didn't feel so much like food as it was a terribly wonderful snack.

I found myself remembering all the other club sandwiches that I had eaten before, usually in cheap diners across the country while my dad was carting us from one state to the next. I picked up a piece of bacon that had fallen out of one side of the sandwich and tucked it between my lips. I couldn't really taste anything but I could almost feel my body breaking down the salt, protein, and fat. I guess I was hungry, even if I couldn't feel it.

"I know it's a stupid question, but how are you feeling?"

I settled back against my pillow and began the process of picking one quarter of my sandwich apart, bread, slathered with mayo to one side meats to the other, and finally swiss cheese. My dad was right, it was a stupid question, but I answered it anyway.

"Tired," I finally said. It was true. I was tired. But it was the kind of tired that sleep couldn't fix. It was the bone deep tired that came when the world had just given me too much to deal with. "Exhausted."

My dad took a seat on the foot of the bed, tucking one sock clad foot beneath him.

"I remember when my dad died. I wasn't very old. Old enough, I guess, to understand that my dad was going to die, young enough to think that it shouldn't be happening to me. I hid in the closet for two days. I don't know why, it made perfect sense at the time."

I found it hard to imagine my dad doing anything of the sort, but he didn't really have a reason to lie to me now. I popped a piece of turkey in my mouth and chewed thoughtfully. I tasted it more than I had the bacon, but only a little. "How did grandma take that?"

"Pretty well, all things considering. I think I was mad at her. Here I was, feeling like my heart got ripped out, and she was still cooking, cleaning, eating, doing all those things that I just didn't want to do anymore. Then again, I never needed an excuse to be mad at my mom."

Yeah, I had picked up on that. Dad and Grandma were not what I would have called close. He seemed to dislike her for being a witch, and therefore himself, and that created a whole lot of weird feelings. I could empathize. I was nothing but one big ball of weird feelings.

"Anyway," my dad continued, watching as I finished off the turkey and moved on to the ham, "I pretty much assumed that she never loved my dad, that it was all some big joke, and she was happier without him."

I knew that wasn't true. I had Grandma's journals. So far as I could tell, she loved my grandfather a lot. I didn't say that right then, though, not only because my dad was clearly working himself up to passing along some life changing epiphany moment, but because interrupting him was just too much energy.

"So it got to the point where she was telling me I needed to eat, or at least take a bath because I smelled exactly how an almost teenage boy who hadn't bothered to bathe would smell. And I just got mad, really mad, I was so angry that I burst out of the closet and accused her of all the terrible things that I had been thinking while sitting alone in the dark." He shook his head, staring down at his lap, lost in his memory. "I was expecting her to yell right back at me. My mom was like that, she didn't take people snapping at her without giving them her own two cents, kind of like you. But she just stood there, she took it, and when I was so red in the face and dizzy with the anger that I couldn't go on any more she just asked if I was going to take a bath or if she ought to dunk me in the lake."

I couldn't help myself, I laughed. Maybe it was the soda getting to my malnourished cells but it struck me as hilarious.

My dad grinned at me. "I know, I know. But her saying that made me realize how dumb I was being. When I just looked up at her, completely shocked, she told me that she had been doing all those things, eating, bathing, and such, because she had me. She couldn't fall apart because I was there, and I needed to be taken care of."

I frowned. I wasn't sure how this was supposed to help me. No one needed me. My dad had never needed me, neither had my mom. My one and only friend had recently started a relationship with a brand-new girlfriend, who was nearly my other friend. The vampires, so far as I could tell, were laying low since one of their own was dead and there was a good chance another one was involved. I didn't have anyone. Just little ol' me, and the ball of sadness that I was wrapped up in.

"Okay," I finally said.

"The world needs you, Lorena."

I blinked, looking past my half-eaten sandwich to stare at my dad, sure that he was being ridiculous. Then I saw the look of absolutely sincerity and pushed my food aside.

"You wanna run that one by me again?"

"Even if you never decide to bring magic into the world the Order of the Loyal Hermit is certainly going to try to do something about this prophecy, and I knew them well enough to know that whatever they plan, it isn't going to be good."

I hadn't thought about that. That made the cold feeling that had grown in my belly turn into a pile of nauseating sludge. "Oh."

"Yeah, that about sums it up."

"What am I supposed to do about it?"

"Getting out of bed would be a good place to start," my dad eyed the debris of my grief.

"And then?"

"A shower."

I rolled my eyes. "Yeah, I get it, basic hygiene is needed, but what then?"

My dad ran a hand through his silver streaked hair. "The way I see it, you've got a few options. You can go to the Vampire House and pick whatever blood sucker will have you and... well..." my dad trailed off.

"Ew, dad, ew. Let's never discuss that again."

He held up his hands, palms outward. "I won't argue with you on that. But it's an option."

I didn't like that option. It wasn't that the vampires that were left weren't great options for the father of the prophecy child. There was Alan, the hottest vampire to ever exist. And there was Dmitri, who had that brooding handsome artist thing going for him. The problem was that sometimes Dmitri's brooding turned into full-on Hulk moments and Alan was desperately in love with him, hulk or not.

Neither made good candidates.

"Okay, next option?"

"You get yourself prepared for Marquessa to return with the army of witches."

That option was not without merit. Marquessa was Jenny's, my one and only friend, grandmother. She had been friends with my grandmother, and was currently wandering the world finding witches who were hopefully going to help us take down the Order of the Loyal Hermit. The Order was my mother's cult and they were the people who were so hard up against me fulfilling my prophecy that their leader, whom I had dealt a serious blow to, had used his magic to try to kill me in my dreams.

"Not a bad choice, but what else?"

"Well, there is always vengeance." My dad shrugged. "Your reasoning would be your own but I've watched enough kung Fu movies to know what happens when the hero loses a loved one."

I laughed again, and felt a little better for it. I had almost forgotten that I didn't completely hate my dad. It was easy to forget, considering everything that had happened. I might hold a grudge, but he didn't win the worst father of the year award.

"So, is your vote for raising the army?"

He leaned over and kissed my forehead. "Honestly? I think you ought to go for vengeance."

CHAPTER TWO

I'd read enough comic books to know exactly how vengeance stories went. A person got angry, they went on a kickboxing rampage, and at the end of it, they regretted everything that they had ever done to get to that last epic battle. Usually that hero had a witty buddy and a centerfold-worthy love interest to keep them going. Me? My buddy was off schmoozing her love interest and my guy? He was dead. No kickboxing rampages for me.

I tried to keep all of those thoughts at bay while I stepped beneath the spray of the first shower I'd had in a week. I had to admit that it felt good. My terrible eating habits and staying in bed had not done wonders for my skin. I used half a bottle of cheap shampoo on my hair in a trio of wash, rinse and repeat. Then I scrubbed myself with a loofah until my skin looked more lobster chic than European pale.

All the while I categorized what I knew, and what I thought.

I had woken up, six and a half days ago, from a near death experience in an evil wizard's coma-induced dreamscape. My father had been there to tell me that Wei was gone, and so was Zane, his vampire brother. There was a good chance that my half-sister, Connie had something to do with it. I don't remember the details, I was pretty much in shock when he told me, but I was piecing it together. Over the next few days I had just lost my energy until I crawled into bed, sure that I wasn't going to get out of it ever again.

The Order had hurt Wei. I was sure of it. The question was, what was I going to do about it?

Kickboxing rampage, that's what. Or, you know, whatever the magical equivalent was. I was going to gear up, and kick in some doors, take some names, and chew bubble gum...or whatever the cliché was. I was going to hurt whoever had taken Wei from me.

I wasn't even sure what it was about him that I liked so much. I certainly had more in common with Dmitri, but there were just some things that I couldn't forgive and being cornered and made to fear for my life in the sanctuary of a library was definitely one of them. But there was something about Wei. He was always so cool, so calm and composed and collected...until we got alone. Then I got to see this secret side of him, this person who could kiss with enough oomph to knock my proverbial socks off, and who could smile and laugh. That was my Wei. It made it somehow more special that only I knew that part of him. Greedy? Maybe. But if I was supposed to have someone's prophecy spawn I was allowed to be greedy about who I got to have it with.

The tears were in my eyes before I even knew it.

I wasn't going to have that little spawn, was I? I wasn't going to give birth to magic. I wasn't sure why that made me so sad. I'd never really been married to the idea in the first place. But now that it wasn't even an option. I was pretty torn up about it.

I slid to the floor and let myself cry while the water pounded down around me. It wasn't just crying. It was a full-on sob. The kind where I couldn't breathe, where I couldn't think, all I could do was feel the tears on my cheeks, hot even with the water on. My head felt dizzy and the food that I'd just barely managed to eat was threatening to come up. It was a hard few minutes before the water finally turned cold enough that I could think again. Then I felt better, more clear headed, and more sure of myself.

I could do this. I had to do this.

When I pulled on a fresh pair of jeans and a clean t-shirt I was feeling a little bit better. Well enough to step out of the bedroom that had been my own personal fortress of solitude and into the little living room that was half cluttered with my grandmother's things, and half cluttered with mine. On no less than three separate occasions I had tried to clear out her stuff, the most recent of which had been just moments after I had heard that Wei was dead, and for all of those she'd been interrupted by her own feelings or an emergency, sometimes both. One day this place would be hers, she'd fought hard enough for it, right? Right.

My dad was standing at the kitchen sink, rinsing out the skillet he had used for the bacon. He didn't use soap, not on real cast iron. Just plenty of hot water to the grease before plopping it down on a burner to warm the water.

"And so she emerges," my father said, not bothering to look over his shoulder, "what's the plan?"

I paused, standing in the center of the living room. The house wasn't all that big. It was one long rectangle with a bedroom on either side. A kitchen and a living room that had nothing but a little table separating one space from the other. Even so I wasn't sure, from this distance, if my father was kidding or not.

In all of my entire life my dad had never asked me what my plan was. He hadn't even asked me about college aspirations or my career of choice. He'd just carted me around from one place to another and made the vast majority of my decisions for me.

"Okay pod person, who are you and what have you done with my father?"

He flicked the heat off the cast iron skillet and turned to look at me. "What?"

"My dad tells me what to do, he doesn't ask me what I want. That's pretty much been the theme of my entire existence up until very, very recently. Now you come in here, being all nice and stuff. You make me my favorite food, you share some of your childhood drama, and you ask me what my plan is? Either you aren't my dad or you are under some kind of spell."

He gave me a long look that I didn't fully understand. I caught some of the emotions in his eyes, sadness, frustration, and something else I couldn't name. Rather than answer me he plucked up a dish towel and began to dry his hands. Then, with all the careful perfection that I knew my father to have, he placed it right back where it was when he had picked it up, right down to the folds.

"There is a chance I may have made a mistake in being the dictator of your life."

Definitely a pod person. My dad wasn't one for apologies either.

"What alternate reality have I stumbled into?" I held my hands out in either direction.

His smile didn't quite reach his eyes, but he took a seat at the dining table and invited me to sit across from him. I hesitated. If my dad really was a pod person, or some evil twin, I didn't really want to know. I did not have the energy to deal with that crisis right this moment. I sat down anyway.

"Lorena, I did everything that I did in order to keep you away from your grandmother, your mother, and the prophecy. Despite all of that. the very first thing you do as an adult is walk headlong into all three. I'm a witch, I should have known better than to keep you from your destiny."

"Yeah, about that. How did I never know you were a witch? What kind of witch are you? Have you been practicing all these years and I just never knew it? I mean, what's the deal here?" The questions spilled out of my mouth in a fast jumble. I hadn't really known how curious I was until they were right there in front of me.

This time the smile did reach his eyes. It was a great big proud smile too. "I am a mathemagician."

Yeah, okay, never mind. This was definitely my dad. No one on the face of the earth could have had something as boring as 'mathemagician' as their title but my very own father.

"A what, now?"

His grin warmed a few degrees. "I use math to cast spells."

"Are you serious?"

He shrugged, looking just the tiniest bit smug. "It's so weird to you? You wouldn't have any issue with me saying I was a cauldron witch, which is basically a chemist, or an ink witch, which is basically a literature witch. Math can't be magical?"

As far as I was concerned math was pretty much the opposite of magic. It was a hell scape from which I had never quite escaped. "How does that work?"

"For me, equations take place of my spell work. Every number has a meaning," he explained, "from 0, which is the number of infinity or infinite choices, to the number nine, which is new paths or binding depending on what's around it. Seven is luck and change, five is...well you get the idea. Keep in mind these are gross oversimplifications to something that is very complex."

"Yeah, okay, sure," I said, pretty sure I was following along. "So, like...alright, you are going to have to explain this to me a little bit better."

His eyes lit up with a true enthusiasm I had rarely ever seen from my dad outside of a sweater vest sale. He grabbed a piece of scratch paper. "It's all about equations. Some spells are very, very simple. Let's do a divination. Now, the number four is considered the number of psychic energy, so that's our goal."

He wrote the number four towards the right side of the paper.

"Now, tell me what you want to know."

Well, to be honest, there was only one thing that was weighing on my mind. "How did Wei die?"

My dad froze, mechanical pencil still in his hand. "Lorena, I-"

"Can you do it?" I asked.

His mouth formed a little line. Some of the enthusiasm had crept out of his eyes. I felt a little guilty about that, but not nearly guilty enough to take it back. Finally, he nodded his head. "Yes, I can."

"Then that's what I want to know."

He took a deep breath and turned his eyes back to the paper. "That's a little more difficult than what the weather might be like tomorrow. But okay. Let's see. I'll need Wei's number."

"His what?" I asked, curiosity getting the better of me. I swear I was part cat.

"Everyone has a number that is specific to them. The most rudimentary way of discovering a number is by adding the numbers of someone's birthday together. Like, if someone was born on May 7th in the year two thousand you would add five, for the fifth month, the seventh, for the seventh day of that month, and two, because when you add the numbers in the year two thousand you just come up with two. And you keep adding your answers together until you come up with a single digit number. In our case here, we'd get fourteen from adding five, seven, and two. And when we had one and four together we get five, which would be that person's number." My father jotted down each equation as he said it, and then circled the number five at the very end.

I gave him a dumb look. "Rudimentary, right."

He shot me a smirk, his eyes lighting up with even more enthusiasm. "Well yes. To be honest, a birthday only means so much, especially where a vampire is concerned. Because they would also have a rebirthday. A better number would be to take the day they were born, the day they died and discover a number based off of those two. And rather than keeping that number to a single digit you would add things together until it was a number between one and twenty-two, since that is the number of numeric mastery."

I had no clue what numeric mastery was, and I thought asking my dad might send him on another tangent from which there could be no escape.

"Okay, but we don't have either one of those dates."

He smiled at me. "We don't need them. Like I said, those are only the basics. People are more than a single number, or a single life path, or whatever you feel like calling it. Those simple numbers are just the basics. We can create a number based off of what we know of him, to be a signifier for him in the mathematical spell."

I nodded, understanding that at least a little bit. "Okay, how do we do that?"

"You tell me three things about him, three core pieces of his personality, and we use the number associated with each. Then, as stated before. We add the numbers together until they are between zero and 22. Now, keep in mind that this has to be something very personal. Not just a good smile or long hair. You have to tell me three things about Wei that are personal, that make up what drives him. In this way, we can create a soul number. Do you know him well enough for that?"

I had to think about that. *Did I?* I'd like to think I knew him well. I did fancy myself in love with the vampire, after all. But did I know him well enough to help my dad make a soul number? Here's hoping.

"He's big into self-perfection. He wants to be strong, inside and out."

My dad nodded. "the number nine correlates with achievement of mind, body, and soul." He jotted that down.

I lapsed into another silence. Wei was far more than a martial arts master looking for perfection of self. He was haunted by his own downfall. He had a lot of misgivings about me and him making a child since he felt like he kind of screwed up with his first wife and kid. To be fair, he kind of did, but he had been young and it wasn't really his fault that she had gone off the deep end...literally.

"Guilt," I finally said. After all it was guilt that drove him into the arms of Vlad the Impaler, father and creator of all...what was it...eleven vampires that walked the earth? The knowledge of that made a knot in my stomach. There were only twelve vampires in the entire world, if you included Vlad. There should have been ten times that. But magic was disappearing, slowly evaporating.

All of the shapeshifters, wolf, bear, and otherwise, created a single clan somewhere in the British Isles, and witches, according to Marquessa, were being born weaker and weaker than the generations before. The only people who didn't seem to be suffering, or at least weren't showing that they were suffering, was the Order of the Loyal Hermit. The creepy cult that my mom and sister belonged to were perfectly okay with the magic getting smaller because they thought that it should only belong to a few anyway. I couldn't bring myself to agree.

My father wrote down the number one next to the number nine. "One more."

I looked down at my lap and said the one word that had been playing over and over again in my head. "Passionate."

My father gave me a look. "Lorena, are you sure? I've met Wei before and..."

I looked up at him now, fixing my eyes with his. I knew Wei. I knew him better than anyone. When he was just with me, when he could be himself without all of those carefully crafted walls, he was beyond passionate. "I'm positive."

My father wrote down the number six. "Okay, we have nine, plus one, plus six. That creates the magical number of sixteen."

I nodded. "So that's less than twenty-two. So now what?"

He placed the number twenty-two towards the left side of the paper, a few spaces away from the number four. I was pretty sure just writing down those two numbers couldn't be all of it. Shock and amazement, I was right.

"Here's where mathemagics gets tricky. We need to get from our soul number here." He used the tip of the pencil to point to the number twenty-two. "And get to the number four, the number for divination. Now, the easiest way is to subtract the number eighteen. But that doesn't work."

"Why?"

"Because the spell uses all the numbers, not just the soul number and the initiate number. The number eighteen, magically speaking, has to do with creative material gain. If we were trying to divine the best way for Wei to get money through his artistic endeavors we'd be set."

God, I hated math. I palmed my chin in both of my hands and felt like I was back in middle school again, staring at Bret Polowski's hair, wondering if the curls were real or if he used a curling iron while Mrs. Haberdasher droned on and on about prime numbers.

"So, what do we do?" I asked.

"We have to get creative. We want to know about the means of his death, right?"

I nodded. "Yeah."

"The number for death is seven."

I frowned. "Wait, I thought seven was about luck?"

He nodded and gave me a smile I might have called proud if it had been on anyone's face but my father's. I had never known him to be proud of me for anything. "It is, but it's also the number for change, and there is no greater change than that from life to death."

He wrote down the number seven next to the sixteen. "Now, to make it more difficult, we have to add these two." He jotted down an addition sign between the sixteen and the seven.

"Because...we are trying to...figure out how? Not...keep him from death?" I hoped.

He gave me that proud smile again. I tried to ignore the happy hum in my chest. I totally didn't need my father's approval for anything. I swear. "That's it exactly. You sure you are a necromancer?"

"I've got the ghost cat to prove it. Okay, so if you add twenty-two and seven, you get twenty-three. Right?"

He nodded. "That you do, and now everything falls into place."

"Why?"

"Because nineteen is the number of all magical occurrences."

I held my breath. Wei's death, as far as I knew, had to be considered a magical occurrence. "So, we subtract that?"

My father nodded, his eyes focused on the paper as he finished off the equation. I don't know what I expected to happen. Bright flashing lights, a sudden shift of numbers on the paper. I wasn't sure, but I was definitely expecting something to happen once my father carefully scribed the equal symbol. What I got was a whole lot of nothing.

"Uhh, is that it?"

My father frowned, holding the paper between two hands as he looked down at the equation, checking and rechecking his math.

"We should get an answer," he said absently.

"Is there a waiting period?"

He shook his head. "It should be immediate, if the equation is correction."

My heart sank. "If?"

He gave me a look. "Lorena, I don't want to lie to you here. I don't want to give you false hope."

I raised my brow at him. "What are you talking about?"

"There are two reasons this didn't work. The first was that the soul number is incorrect."

I thought about that. Self-perfection, guilt, and passion? No. I was one hundred percent sure that those were the core of who Wei was as a person. I knew it the way I knew the back stories for everyone in the Justice League, okay, maybe not everyone, but at least the core members.

"It's right. What's the other reason?"

He looked away as if he didn't want to tell me. "That he's not dead."

CHAPTER THREE

I stood up from the table so fast that my chair slapped against the floor.

"What are you doing?" my dad asked.

"I'm going to find my boyfriend."

I turned away from the table and the scribbled equations, and stomped to where my jacket was. It was cold in the mountains this time of year, and I was going to need a jacket. I shoved one arm and then the other into the sleeves. I didn't know what I was going to do. I didn't even have the first glimpse of a plan, but I knew that I was not just going to sit here and hope that Wei wasn't dead and that he'd find his way back to me.

"Lorena, wait."

I shook my head. "Nope, not waiting."

My dad reached out for me but I jerked out of his grasp before he could latch on. "Lorena, please."

"Please what?" I demanded, whirling on him. I don't know what he saw in my face but it was enough to make him square his shoulders in preparation for a confrontation. Did he want a fight? I hoped so. I wanted to fight. I wanted to fight with everyone. I didn't understand right then why I was so mad but on a scale of one to volcano I was Mount Saint Helens.

"Please sit down and think about this? Please give it some time? I don't know if you've noticed, Dad, but I've wasted a whole lot of time being a moping little brat who had given up. I could have... damnit, I could have rescued him a week ago if I had known that he wasn't dead. But guess what? I trusted you when you told me that Wei was dead. I trusted you and I don't even know why, since you spent eighteen years lying to me about pretty much everything."

Oh, I guess that's why I was so pissed off.

His face turned a faint pink. Right then it wasn't that big of a deal, but I knew my dad, it would turn red sooner or later and that's when I knew he was really pissed off. I had a knack for pissing him off.

"Now wait just a minute. I've apologized for that."

I scoffed. "Yeah, you have. And hey, look at that, just like magic it's all better again, right? Wrong. Saying you are sorry does not make up for eighteen years of keeping secrets and lying. Sorry isn't a magic word that scrubs the slate clean. Sorry is the first step to making things better. You wanna know what the second step will be?"

The pink had already begun to turn the shade of a tomato. "What's that?" he asked through gritted teeth.

"Getting the hell out of my way. I've got a vampire to rescue."

He didn't get out of my way. Shock and amazement. "Lorena, we need more information. If you want to believe that he is alive, that's fine, but we still need to know where he is and what we are up against."

I hated, absolutely hated, that he was right. I wanted to get the last word in and I wanted to be petty enough to slam the door on my way out. But he was right. Even if I went charging out of that door right that moment I had nowhere to go. Yeah, I could have gone to the Vampire House with the knowledge that their brother wasn't dead after all. And yeah, I could have gone over to Jenny's and asked for her help, even though she'd been absent for about a week and I was kinda mad about that. I had options, but they weren't all that great.

"What do you suggest? More mathemagics?" I asked, waving my hand towards the paper.

He nodded. "Yes, I do. I can do it by myself. In fact, it's probably better if I do. This is going to take time, Lorena. I understand that you want to go charging off after Wei, but we need to know things so you don't get hurt or accidentally get him killed or any one of a thousand bad possible scenarios."

"What am I supposed to do?" I snapped. "Sit around and wait? I've done plenty of that, thank you."

He shook his head. "Get back up, get some training in, and gear up."

He was telling me what to do again and I didn't particularly like it, but what else was I supposed to do? Ignore it completely? No thanks. I needed some kind of direction and even if it came from him right now, I was going to take it.

With a sigh, I picked up my keys. My dad's shoulders sagged.

"You are leaving anyway?"

I shook my head, and then I thought better of it and nodded. "Yeah, I am, but I'm going to do that reinforcement thing. If I hang out here I'm going to go crazy and you need to concentrate on that whole math thing." I scooped up my cell phone. "Text me when you know something."

I walked out of the house, and into the cool night air. I didn't even know that Maahes was following me until I felt the humming weight of the presence of his ghost form on my shoulder. I was grateful for it.

"Hey cat, you ready for this?" I asked.

The cat nudged my ear and I took that as a yes. I'd always wanted a cat. I just always thought he'd be alive when I got him. Silly me.

I yanked open my car door, plopped myself inside, and tore out of the driveway with the Guardians of the Galaxy soundtrack blasting as I drove. It was too cold to put the windows down, but I did it anyway. It wasn't going to bother Maahes and I seriously needed the fresh air. I was mad. I was so mad that I didn't even think about where I was going, I just drove.

The roads of mountainous Virginia wove their way around one curve and into the next. I took them, going sixty miles an hour as the music pounded down around me. I wasn't the world's best driver, but I was close, and anger gave my driving skill a hard edge it might otherwise not have had.

How dare my dad assume that I didn't know Wei. Just because he had met him before didn't mean that he knew him. How dare he not just, for once in my life, trust me. He'd never trusted me. Heck, I was wearing the clothes he picked out for me right up until high school and even then, it had been a struggle to just get him to let me be.

But it wasn't just dad that I was mad at. It was everyone. It was Alan and Dmitri, it was Jenny and Reikah. It was Marquessa and my mother and my sister and Zane. Hell, I was even mad at me. I was a lot mad at me and that didn't make me feel any better about any of it.

If I hadn't been so wrapped up in my own sorrow I would have thought to double check on Wei long before this moment. The fact that I didn't was all on my shoulders and that hurt more than anything else could. I pulled over in an empty and abandoned gas station parking lot and gave over to the tears that had nearly blinded me.

Two sob fests in one day, I thought as I swatted the glove compartment open to retrieve a pile of whisper-thin take out napkins.

I hated myself for letting my feelings get the best of me. Not just the tears, but everything. I could have been doing a thousand things since I woke up from that stupid dreamscape. I could have been training. I could have been reconnecting with my dad. I could have finished up making the house all my own like I'd been meaning to do for like...forever. I could have been busy but instead I had been wallowing, drowning in a self-made pool of pity and guilt and everything else.

I knew, logically, that depression, the situational kind and the general kind, couldn't be helped. That the brain did whatever it wanted to do. But logic had no place in sob session number two.

I was almost startled when Maahes crawled into my lap. Sometimes Maahes had all the weight of a ghost, something that I could feel with my mind but not my skin, but right now he was as heavy as a real live cat. His dark back paws settled on my thighs and he lifted himself up so that his front paws were on my chest. He stretched himself up until his little nose was almost up against mine. It was the strangest thing that I had ever seen a cat, ghost or otherwise, do. His nose pressed lightly to mine in the words smallest 'boop' of affection, and I felt better.

I knew cats weren't big into hugs, but I wrapped my arms around the tangible ghost anyway and gave him a hug. Rather than pull away, or disappearing like I expected him to, he curled over my arm and started to purr. It wasn't a normal purr, like your average everyday cat, but Maahes wasn't average. The purr seemed to reverberate right through me, a happy hum that went soul deep. A few minutes later all of the sick and angry emotions I had felt faded.

My dad made mistakes. Yup, that was true, but he had fessed up to them and he was trying to make up for it now. Marquessa was trying to bring me an army, and I certainly couldn't fault her for that. There was a good chance the Alan and Dmitri were just as wrapped up in their own misery as I had been. And Jenny? Well, I didn't know what her excuse was, but I was going to have to hear it out, because she was my friend and I deserved to know what was going on and where she had been.

I gave Maahes one final pat, silent thanks for what he had done, and adjusted him so that I could drive. When I started the car up this time around I had a better idea of where I was going and what I was doing. It was eleven o'clock. Prime vampire time, and there were a couple of vampires I knew who could probably be cheered up with the news of Wei being alive.

~~

The old Victorian mansion that operated as the home for the Sons of Vlad was a dream. Especially now, with a dusting of snow on the ground and the moonlight glittering on the two dozen windows sprinkled over three floors. It was worthy of a painting, or at least a high-quality Christmas photo. The driveway, however, was cluttered with half a dozen sleek black cars, all bearing expensive names and foreign license plates. I wondered what on earth was going on here. Was it a party? If it was I certainly wasn't invited.

Growing up, thanks to all the moving around, I had never been what you would call popular. I hadn't gotten invited to much, and my dad probably wouldn't have let me go even if I had. I did not have the gumption to walk into something that I hadn't been invited to.

I was about two seconds away from driving away and coming back later when the door opened and Alan stepped out. If it had been anyone else I might have still driven away but Alan was my friend in the way that only he could be.

He looked like an angel, though he always did, wearing a black velvet doublet and black slacks, pressed to the kind of perfection that my father aspired to. Even his shirt, flouncing with lace, was black as pitch. In fact, the only thing of color about him was his hair. A perfect fall of blonde that he had pulled into a rigorous braid.

I could see how tired he was from here, even before he lifted one arm and placed it on one of decorative pillars. He buried his face against the crook of his arm and took on that unnatural stillness that only vampires could have. Something was not okay.

I opened the car door and he jerked to attention. I slid out of the front seat and his eyes went wide at seeing me. He looked over his shoulder at the front door, and then back to me.

"Lorena? What are you doing here?" His voice was a quiet hiss. I knew he was upset because I could hear his native French in his words. Alan rarely ever sounded French. Yeah, something was definitely wrong.

"I have news, I came to see you."

He shook his head, making his braid lash back and forth behind him. "You shouldn't be here right now, Lorena. This is not a good time. I will come to you when things are...better."

I shook my head. This wasn't like Alan at all. He rarely ever used my name, preferring French pet names to my Christian one. First, my dad being nice and now Alan giving me the brush off? I was beginning to believe my alternate reality theory had more credence than I originally thought. Then again, maybe I had never really woken up from that dreamscape after all. Wei was dead after all, maybe this was a nightmare. Ohhh no, there was a line of thought I just couldn't take myself down. No need to always be wondering if I was awake or asleep. That was just asking for lunacy.

"Alan, what's going on? I need to talk to you. And to Dmitri. My dad and I figured something out."

He put his hand on my shoulder and pushed me back to his car. For all the strength behind that movement it was a graceful dismissal. Alan was always graceful.

"Alan, what's-"

"Little brother? What is this?" It was a woman's voice, soft and musical and tinged ever so lightly with the French accent that Alan only had when he was befuddled or upset.

Alan went completely and totally still. His eyes went wide, showing the full ring of his perfect irises and he swallowed. It had to have been a reflexive movement because vampires, unless they were sucking down blood, didn't need to swallow.

Curiosity drew my eyes away from Alan and to a woman I could only guess was his sister. She was dressed in a long flowing gown of black, with the kind of overdone layers that you only saw in historical films. The black suited her, just like it suited Alan, showing off her perfectly pale skin and golden curls. She, just like her brother, looked angelically beautiful. Her shoes made the kind of stiff clack that you only got when you wore heels as she approached. Her pale hands clutched an elegant fan that she unfurled with a practiced flick of her wrist.

"Alan? Will you not introduce me to your friend?"

Up close she was even prettier than her brother, and I honestly did not know that was possible. Her eyelashes were so pale and fine they looked like tiny silver fans around eyes so perfectly blue I was pretty sure I could drown in them. There was the faintest tinge of rose in her cheeks, a sign that she had fed recently enough to give her a glimmer of life that she might otherwise not have had.

I could see by the tightness of his jaw that this was something that Alan absolutely didn't want to do. I was confused. Usually Alan was the paragon of courtly manners. This was not those.

"Alan?" I asked, hoping that my confusion wasn't as obvious as it felt.

He didn't sigh, vampires didn't really need to do that, instead his eyes closed for a moment as if he could blink away whatever it was that was bothering him. When they opened again they were cool and clear and empty.

"Lorena, may I introduce my sister, Genevieve, my sister and the third wife to Vlad, father of all vampires. Genevieve, my dearest sister, may I introduce Lorena Quinn, granddaughter of Loretta Queen the Prophetess."

Genevieve. I knew that name, and it solidified what I had already guessed. His sister was here, and judging by all those cars she was not alone. Their clothes suggested that they were mourning Wei. Unless of course vampires just bedecked themselves in black whenever they got together. I wasn't willing to take that idea off the table just yet.

"Pleasure to make your acquaintance," I said, trying my best not to sound like a complete bumpkin. I don't know why I bothered, in comparison to her I was going to look like a bumpkin no matter what I did.

She shook her head, making the perfect curls around her face bounce. "Oh no, the pleasure is all mine." She said it with such complete sincerity that I found myself smiling at her in spite of myself. Her accent was lighter than her brothers, more delicate. Then she placed a single finger to the very corner of her lip and tilted her head so that she looked like the perfect bridal doll. "However, I do believe my brother has been derelict in his announcements of you. Are you not also a necromancer?"

She said the word necromancer like I might have said outbreak monkey, with a mixture of disgust and fascination. Having it come from her smiling mouth was a double slap to my face.

"Uhhhh," I managed to get out that syllable and no other before another face darkened the still open doorway. I hoped they had enough money to pay the electric bill. Who was I kidding? Of course, they did.

This face I knew, almost as well as Alan's. Dmitri was a massively built man, with the kind of shoulders that would have made a football coach drool. His hair, prone to glorious curls, were in every shade of black and brown imaginable, making them look more like a pelt than actual hair. He had done something with it to make it slick, and had pulled it back into a careful knot at the back of his neck. That was almost as strange as Alan being rude. As far as I could tell Dmitri never wore his hair, which was prone to curl riotously, back, much less held in place by what looked like impressive amounts of product.

"Alan, Genevieve, Vlad is ready for...Lorena?" When he'd started off talking his voice had been careful, precise, and utterly empty of feeling. I had never known Dmitri to be empty of feeling. In fact, part of my problem with him had been the fact that he was prone to having just a little bit too much in the feeling department. He was a brooding artist after all. But he didn't show anything in his voice until he got to my name, which was gasped out with the shock of someone who both did not expect and didn't want to be saying what they were.

I felt thoroughly unwanted. Great.

"Gee guys, I didn't realize you hated me that much." I shoved my hands in my pockets.

Alan gave me a look. "We could never hate you, Lorena."

"Not at all," Dmitri promised.

"It is simply not a good time for you to be here," Alan finished.

Genevieve raised a perfect pale brow up her equally perfect forehead. "And why not?"

The male vampires clapped their mouths shut, refusing to look at either myself nor Genevieve. I was beginning to think that maybe they were right. Maybe I shouldn't be here. Something weird was going on and I had enough weird going on in my life.

"You have spent a rather intriguing amount of time promising us that we would be right in trusting this little witch, my brother," Genevieve said, lifting her chin imperiously. She didn't look so much like a bridal doll as that of the wicked queen from a fairy tale. "And yet it seems as if you would deprive us of actually getting to know her."

Wait, what? There were a lot of things about that statement that I didn't much like, starting with "little witch" and ending with the way she looked right at me as she said it. I found myself tucking my thumbs in my belt loops because I didn't want to do anything rude with my hands. Keeping them in my pockets just wasn't enough.

"Lorena can be trusted," Alan said. He turned and offered his sister the charming smile that I was used to being pointed in my general direction.

"Then perhaps she should say so herself."

Yet another voice. I was getting pretty tired of vampires and their sneaky capabilities. Batman, master of the stealthy entrance, had nothing on these guys. This voice was not feminine, or soft like Genevieve's. In fact, it was pretty much the opposite. It boomed with the strength and power of a commander, and was rich with the melodic accent of a distant mountainous land.

I couldn't see whomever was talking. Dmitri had shifted his body just enough to put himself between me and the speaker. That was just a tad disquieting, especially since Alan moved to do the same. Dmitri, was the protective sort, sometimes a little too protective. I had never known Alan to put himself in harm's way. How big of a threat was this person that I needed not one, but two vampires to keep me safe? Answer? Too big for my britches.

And yet, my traitorous mouth was moving before I could stop myself. "I do say so."

Alan winced. Dmitri stiffened. And I knew that I had just made a very poor life decision.

"Is that what you say, Lorena Quinn?" he asked. He didn't sound happy about it. "Move aside, sons of my blood. Let me see this mortal creature that you have put such faith in that you would offer your own backs to me."

Apparently, I was not the only one to notice the wall of flesh that had been offered up to protect me. Goodie. Alan gave me a look of apology before stepping to the side.

Vlad the Impaler, because who else could he be, was not so large as I would have imagined, nor was he as buff. When I pictured a heroic leader of an army that won against insurmountable odds and spawned a myth, a whole slew of novels, and a bunch of movies to be made after him I had to picture someone titanic in build. He couldn't have been a few inches taller than me, and he wasn't all that muscular either.

He looked to be around my dad's age, mid to late forties. He was fit, but not intimidating in build, even a little soft around the middle. His long dark hair flowed in rich waves around an angular, not entirely unattractive face. I wondered why his hair got to be down while the other men had theirs pulled back. It was his eyes though, that saved him from being plain. They were dark, richly so, like shadows captured in his gaze. In fact, the more I looked at him the better he looked.

He walked in sure, even steps until he stopped right in front of me, leaving me with barely more than a couple inches of personal space. I could feel, rather than see, the tension radiating off of Alan and Dmitri.

Being a necromancer, I have a leg up on understanding the undead. I knew that Alan and Dmitri were very much not okay with what was happening. It wasn't just the body language. It was a sense. I knew that Genevieve was also tense, but it didn't have the same desire to protect as what was coming from the other two. There was something else going on with her that I didn't fully understand. Vlad, however, was watching me with the intensity that the cobra spared its dinner.

"You are prettier than they led me to believe," he said, reaching out and brushing a hand through my hair, "younger, too. When they spoke of you I pictured a woman fully formed and grown, not this fascinating creature who has a foot in both youth and maturity."

Ick? Like, I didn't have a problem with being young, but there was something about the way that he was focusing on my apparent age that made me wanna take a few steps back. I was, of course, far too proud and just a dash too scared to do that.

"Thanks?"

He smiled, and his whole face changed. I liked a good smile, the kind that could be on a Colgate commercial or some other grin-centric add campaign. Wei had an incredible smile. Vlad? His was something else. He went from a five to a ten. That's how good it was. I found myself blinking just to make sure I wasn't imagining anything. Nope. Great smile. A plus.

"You are very welcome." He lifted one of my hands, which I don't even remember him taking, and brought it to his lips. They were softer than they should have been. I blinked and shook my head. The tension coming off of Genevieve went up a few notches.

"What's going on?" I asked.

"We are mourning the passing of our beloved Wei, would you do me the honor of joining us?" he made it sound like I was getting invited to Cinderella's ball.

"Uhhh," was all I managed to say before I heard an ungodly screech echoed around me.

A moment later a form slammed into me. I say form rather than person because I was pretty sure that the form wasn't entirely human in shape. It moved quick and hit hard and I tumbled down to the ground, my newly washed jeans getting some impressive grass stains on the legs.

"Nooo!" the shrill voiced screeched again. The person grabbed my arm and jerked it hard enough that my teeth clacked together.

"Yasmina! Stop this!" someone yelled, I think it was Dmitri but I was too busy seeing stars as a She-Hulk sized elbow slammed into my gut. The air whooshed out of my lungs and tears sprang into my eyes. I was hurting pretty bad.

"You will not take him away from us! He cannot have you!" the she-beast screamed at me. Claws as long as my arm swept at me, I got my arm up in time to take the strike anywhere else but the chest shot she was aiming for. Jeez what was she planning? To dig out my heart? She struck with the other hand and I realized that was exactly what she was planning.

I had spent months training with Wei, and he had been a harsh taskmaster where the martial arts were concerned. The forms he had taught me relied on using my opponent's strength against them. Good. If that was as true as I hoped it was this fight was in the bag. This chick had a whole lot of strength.

I used my legs to arch up off the ground and roll to one side. The female, Yasmina if I could believe what everyone was yelling at her, lunged at me again, but this time I was ready. I rolled onto my back again and caught her movement with my feet using a push to carry her over my head and send her tumbling.

I did not have time to revel in a perfectly executed throw, because she was after me in a blur of speed that would have left Superman eating dust. She slammed into my back, sending me right back to the ground, this time on my front. I got a nice mouthful of carefully manicured lawn. Her claws raked down my back and I admit it, I screamed.

"I will lap the blood from your cooling flesh once you are dead," she whispered in my ear. Well, that was vivid. Over dramatic, maybe, but vivid.

"Yasmina, stop!" I head Alan say.

I heard, rather than saw, movement. A heavy weight hit Yasmina in the side. She didn't budge. I turned my neck just enough to see that Yasmina held Alan by the throat. It was too dark and my head hurt too much to get a good look at her. He was snarling and swiping at her, but I knew, even with the delicate claws at the ends of his fingers, that he was no fighter. Besides, the Brides of Vlad seemed to be in a league of their own where ability was concerned.

She tossed Alan aside like he was a sack of flour. He went tumbling. I heard the sound of fabric ripping and I knew that Alan was going to be upset. He really liked his clothes. Heck, I was gonna be upset. They had been really nice clothes.

"Do not protect this whore."

Okay, that was it. In the past three months people had been making a lot of assumptions about me and the three hims and what I was going to do with said hims and I was pretty much over it. On top of that I was still nursing the last few bits of my sob inducing anger and I had no time to swallow them down. I was a necromancer and I was going to show this crazy vampire just what that meant.

Magic burst out of me like a fist. It rushed up and opened fingers that were not fingers to create what I could only call a ghostly shield around me. The attacker was flung backwards, arcing high into the air and landing on the ground hard enough to leave a divot. If she, and I was ninety-nine percent sure it was a she, was hurt I was pretty much okay with that.

"Yasmina?" Vlad stood to one side of a pretty column, looking down at the dark pile.

"I'm fine," I croaked, "thanks for asking."

No one approached me. I wasn't all too surprised by the fact that the new vampires didn't, but I was a little surprised that understandably protective Alan and Dmitri were keeping their distance. As I looked around I realized that people were either looking on the woman on the ground with various states of pity, or looking at me with equally various states of frightful awe.

"What?" I asked.

Genevieve looked the least afraid, in fact she looked pretty impressed. "I have never seen a spectral shield that strong."

"She is a necromancer," Alan half coughed as he sat up from his place on the grass. He gave his torn sleeve a frown. Told you that he was going to be hissy about it. "She is a woman born of prophecy. Did you think her magic would be small?"

The words sounded a little rude to me, but brother and sister shared the kind of look that held a wealth of amused secrecy.

"It is most impressive," Vlad said, standing on the very edge of the aura of my magic, "I wonder if you can release it as easily as you summoned it."

I honestly had no idea, but I wasn't even going to try until I knew for sure that my attacker wasn't going to be starting things up again.

"I'll answer that question once she is done with her hissy fit," I said.

"You have my word that she will not attack you again."

I nearly scoffed. "Yeah, I don't think I'll be accepting that, considering you did absolutely nothing to stop her in the first place."

Amusement flickered in Vlad's dark eyes and it made me dislike him a little more. I didn't like it when people laughed at my anger, much less my pain, and that look was just a touch shy of a belly laugh.

"As you wish."

Yasmina stirred a few moments later. She sat up and I got my first clear view of the woman who, by the way, apparently wanted to drink the blood from my corpse.

She wasn't a particularly tall woman. She was probably shorter than I was, which was saying something, but she was rounder than me. A few decades ago someone might have called her pleasantly plump, today she might be called fluffy. She wasn't obese, just round, and pretty. Then again, I had yet to see an ugly vampire. She had golden eyes, creamy skin, and the kind of brown hair that had red highlights in it.

"Keep that shield in place as long as you can stand it," she spat at me with the kind of hatred that took years to build, "you seek to take him from us. I will not allow it."

"Who?" I demanded. "Wei?" It was a stupid answer, but the only one I could think of right then. The only vampire I wanted to take away from anything my grumpy and secretive one.

Her pretty face twisted with anger. "Have you not done that already?"

No. I hadn't, but I didn't have the chance to say that.

"Yasmina, you will stop this childish nonsense right this moment." Vlad's voice boomed with power. It wasn't just that he had been some kind of warrior commander, it was the weight of a true vampire, the first of their kind. It was magic, pure and simple, that rippled across the clearing. All of the undead went to their knees automatically. I felt it through my shield and even with that up I had a problem staying up.

"I...I only did it for you," she simpered.

A terrible thought wove through my head, one so ridiculous that I refused to even give it the brain power to finish forming.

"Yasmina, you will go to your rooms and stay there," Vlad ordered.

Her big golden eyes went wide. I was pleased that her hair was messed up. I had done that. Sure, I hadn't done much else, but at least I had managed that. Her lower lip quivered as she said, "but...the mourning dinner."

"You are no longer invited," he explained with harsh simplicity. "You will have to mourn in private."

They kept saying the word 'mourn' like it had a lot of meaning that I just didn't understand.

"What of her?" she snarled, slapping a hand in my general direction.

"She will take your place."

She looked like a kicked puppy. I was so shocked that the shield I had been holding up flickered away. I could see Yasmina consider finishing what we had started but a harsh command from Vlad in a language I didn't know sent her scampering inside, shooting daggers from her eyes at me the entire time.

Vlad approached me and took my hand in his once more. "Forgive my second bride, she was once a princess of her people and has never forgotten it."

He tucked my recently kissed hand into his arm and led me slowly into the mansion that had been, for a very brief time, my home. Without saying a word, the small crowd, minus Yasmina, fell into step behind us. I guess I didn't have a whole lot of choice.

"I... uuhhhh...I'm not really dressed for this, and red isn't really my color."

I held up my wounded arm, blood coated the skin. The scratch hadn't been as deep as I thought, but I was pretty sure my back was terrible.

Vlad looked at the blood on my arm. Not just looked. But stared. His shadow-dark eyes looked it over the way another person might have looked at some fantastic cleavage, or a really impressive set of abs. I lowered my arm. He looked away, but not without licking his lips first. Ew.

"Yes, it would be best if you prepared yourself."

"I will attend her," Genevieve said, stepping forward.

Vlad gave her a hard expression. "That is the job of a servant."

He said servant like it was a bad word. Genevieve bowed her head, but didn't give in. There were just some women who could use submissiveness like a shield.

"Peter is busy preparing our food, and I do not wish to start too late. Already our festivities have been put on hold. Besides, I wish to know the woman whom my brother speaks so well of."

I wasn't sure I wanted her to know me, but my back was beginning to really hurt. I must have made some sound because Vlad sighed in disgust and waved us away.

"Do not dawdle."

Dawdle? Really?

"We will take only as long as we need," Genevieve said with a smile. It was a sneaky answer. I got the feeling that Genevieve was just a sneaky person in general.

She took me gently by the arm and lead me upstairs. The path we took was pretty familiar. We stopped in front of what had once been my room. She pushed the door open and I knew that someone else had moved in. I was guessing, by the lacy dresses that hung up here and there, that it was Genevieve. I wasn't sure how I felt about her living in the place that used to be mine. I focused on the "used to be" part and let her lead me into the massive bathroom.

"You will need to remove your tunic."

Tunic? I mean...really? How removed from reality where these people? I had spent a lot of time with Wei, Alan, and Dmitri. Despite a severe r lack of pop culture knowledge, which I did my absolute best to fix, they were pretty up and up in the culture of modern humanity. Dawdle and tunic where just not words I was used to hearing.

"Okay." I tugged my shirt off, which was totally ruined, and laid it over the sink. I used the triple mirror to get a look at myself. The scratches were just below my bra line, and they were pretty wicked. They could have been worse, but I was pretty sure that they were going to need stitches.

"Sit," she said, pointing a single finger towards the toilet seat. "I will attend you."

I blinked. "Uh, I don't know how to say this without being rude...but I don't think you can help."

She gave me a bland look. "I am quickly forming the opinion that a great deal of what you say will be both rude and honest. While I cannot express pleasure in the former, the latter is a refreshing thing to hear, and thus will forgive that transgression." She waved towards the seat again. "However, while Yasmina has a gift for wounding, I have a gift for mending. Please, sit."

I don't know if it was the pain, the fancy words, or the please that had me plopping myself down, but I did it. I straddled the seat backwards and laid my head down until my forehead touched cool porcelain. A moment later her cool fingers touched my back. I expected my raw skin to burn from her touch. It didn't, in fact the coolness was soothing. Then I felt a hint of magic.

"A vampire who can heal?" I said.

"It is a useful trick when there is little food to choose from, especially in times when minds are small."

There was a whole story in that sentence, but I didn't have the time to ask her about it, because she kept talking.

"I wish that I had been here when Wei went missing. I could have found him. I could have helped him."

"You still can," I blurted. I was struck silent as a sudden freezing sensation spread over my back. I felt my muscles twitch. Then it came to an immediate halt.

"What?" she demanded. Her voice was rich with feeling.

I turned as much as my current position would allow. "Wei isn't dead. Missing, yes, but not dead. I came here tonight to get Alan and Dmitri's help to find him. But...well...then all this nonsense happened and here we are."

She took my chin in her hands. They were still cool. "There is honesty in your eyes."

I frowned at her. "Uh, yeah? Why would I lie about that?"

She turned my head more and I was forced to stand up. I wasn't a tall woman by anyone's standards, but I had to look down at her. She was so dainty, so petite. "You care for him."

I shifted uncomfortably. I hadn't really admitted that to anyone before. And, you know, the first time I said it I kinda wanted it to be to Wei himself, not standing half naked in a bathroom with blood on my arm and my back to a vampire lady. Just saying.

Her smile was small, but warm. "Oh, you poor thing." It disappeared instantly and she gripped my arm. "You cannot say anything to Vlad of this."

I winced. Her grip relaxed, but I pulled away anyway. "Jeez, what the heck?"

She shook her head and pursed her lips. "Wash. I will find you a dress."

No amount of coaxing could get her to elaborate on what she had said. With no other choice, I took a quick shower, my second one of the day. I didn't cry this time. I considered that to be a step in the right direction. I changed into the dress she offered, and within half an hour followed her downstairs.

CHAPTER FOUR

The lights had been dimmed. Dark fabric tossed over lamps and shades alike, until the entire mansion was cast in muted brilliance. I had always loved the way the mansion looked, the walls and floors were made out of all of these rich woods, and the decorating had been elegant. I knew most of the pictures that hung on the walls were of Dmitri's creation, and that it had been Wei who had carved the banisters. My fingers lingered there, as if touching the carving would bring me closer to him.

I was lead to a room I recognized but hadn't spent a whole lot of time in. The formal dining room. Most of my meals had been taken sitting at the little table in the kitchen while I talked with Peter, the major domo and butler to the mansion. He was nowhere to be seen, but there were plenty of other faces.

As far as I could tell, just about all of the vampires were here. Vlad, his three brides, the daughters of the three brides, and Alan and Dmitri all moved to sit along the long dark wood table. I wondered if Wei had carved this too.

"My brides, my daughters," Vlad said as all eyes turned to me, "this is Lorena Quinn, the witch that we have heard so much about." He got up and linked his arm through mine as if in some formal introduction. Then again, I was wearing about ten yards of blue velvet. This was about as formal as it got. Why I got to wear blue and everyone else wore black, I didn't know.

Yeah, okay. What was up with that? What had been said about me and, better question, why? I swallowed hard while I looked into one face and then the next, doing my absolute best to put a name to a person. Once upon a time, on a very nice date with Alan, he had told me the names of all of his vampire brethren. I was really struggling to remember them now.

"You will join us for our meal."

I would? I thought as he maneuvered me around the table. Again, I got the feeling that I didn't have a whole lot of choice. Also, while I knew that vampires could eat, I also knew that they didn't actually gain any nutrition from partaking of mortal food. So, what on earth were they going to be serving for this meal? I had a terrible image of some poor human just being carted out for everyone to eat from. I wasn't sure I could handle that. No, scratch that. I was absolutely positive that I couldn't handle that.

I was led to a seat on the left at the head of the table and even though I had never attended a fancy dinner party before I was pretty sure that was a big deal, mostly because of the mix of emotions the vampires were sending all over the room as Vlad pulled out the chair for me. I glanced around, and saw faces that were either blank or filled with open contempt. Oh goodie.

"Please, sit."

It sounded more like a command than a request, but I sat anyway. I had to admit I was pretty curious about everyone and with everyone here, I needed only to make my announcement once. Yeah, okay, Genevieve had told me not to, but if someone wasn't going to bother telling me why I needed to do something I was far less inclined to obey.

With militant efficiency, Vlad had me sitting in the chair and tucked up to the table in one smooth move. I had almost forgotten that he was, historically speaking, a military leader. I don't know how.

"Welcome to our table," said the woman across from me. "I am Anja." Her hair and eyes were as dark and rich as Vlad's, but she didn't need a smile to look like a ten. She looked to be a few years older than myself, with skin so pale that I could have followed her veins from her neck to her toes if I had the chance. The black gown she wore came all the way up to her collar bone, and a wide choker of rich velvet covered a good portion of her neck.

"Thank you," I responded.

She nodded her head, but didn't bother to say anything else.

"Where will I sit?"

Genevieve was standing in the doorway, her dark fan snapped closed against her palm. Her face held a perfect emptiness, but even so I could feel tension radiating off of her like a plucked wire. What was she so upset about? She'd been upset ever since she told me not to tell Vlad about Wei.

"You will sit by your brother."

I glanced down the line of the table and saw that Alan was pretty much at the other end of the table. She looked at Vlad, looked at the empty seat, and looked at me. I didn't need necromancer senses to know she wasn't totally okay with that arrangement. It was okay, I wasn't comfortable with it either. I'd much rather sit next to Alan.

"I-" I started to say. I already had one vampire bride pissed off at me, I didn't want another one.

"You are a guest in this house, and a bearer of prophecy. It is your right to sit at my left hand."

Yeah, that sounded a lot more important than I felt. I gave Genevieve a look that told her how sorry I was, but she wasn't looking at me anymore. She glided gracefully around to her new seat, pausing until Alan helped her into it.

"Well, that was fascinating." The woman to my left said, her voice purring and rich.

This woman had skin the color of gold dust, not too dissimilar from Wei's, but the rest of her looked more like Reikah. Her long straight hair was held back with a small scrap of black and gold material and the wrapped dress she wore had the markings of a very expensive sari. She also wore more jewelry than I had ever seen in my lifetime, including a length of golden chain that went from her nose to her ear. Her wrists jingled with a wealth of bracelets as she reached out to take my chin in her hand. She looked deep into my eyes and for a moment I was pretty sure she was going to kiss me.

"Ahh, there it is, the spark of prophecy," she said, still keeping her eyes riveted on mine. "Yes, Lorena Quinn, I see it in you. What do you plan on doing about it?"

"Uhhhh," I, master of the monosyllable, said.

"I'm Rehema." She dropped her hand from my chin as quickly as I held it. "I am the daughter of Anja and Vlad."

"Rehema is a prophetess," Vlad said with a great deal of pride before moving to his own seat.

"She's also a tad arrogant if ya dinnae pick up on that already" said another woman. This one pale and red headed. Her voice lilting with the rhythm of one of the British Isles. It wasn't quite Scottish, nor Irish, but something that fell in between. "and she hogs all the wine."

Rehema shrugged her shoulder, completely unrepentant, her lips quirked into a little grin. "Seeing the future takes a toll on the spirit, if a little wine helps, I'll enjoy it."

As if on cue, Peter came out from a door I hadn't noticed before, a decanter in his grip. He paused for a nanosecond as his eyes landed on me but he did not offer me his usual happy greeting before he began to pour out a glass of rich red wine for everyone. Well, everyone but me.

"Uhh, Peter," I said, finally speaking up, "I...uhh...you forgot me."

Peter bowed his head so low I could see the top of it. That was also weird. Peter never bowed to me, not like that. He was more my friend than my servant.

"He will bring you something else," Vlad snapped.

I blinked in confusion. It was Peter who explained. "I do not believe blood wine will be to your taste."

Oh. Right. Blood wine. "Thank you, Peter."

"Do not thank a servant for doing their job," Vlad commanded me.

I frowned. I had worked in fast food. I wasn't okay with that kind of mentality, but when I opened my mouth to say just that a hand liberally decorated with rings wrapped tightly around my wrist in warning. I was surprised enough that I didn't get a moment to say whatever it was that I had been planning to, as the final guest for this unnecessary dinner came in.

She was beautiful. Okay, all the vampires were beautiful, but this one more so, maybe more so because she wasn't wearing the required black. She had the features of a Native American, with a broad square face and sharp nose. Her black hair was plaited into two rich braids, each wrapped in a piece of leather that had been sewn with beads. Her entire outfit had the same intricate bead work, so that the simple leather dress she wore glittered with every move. Her bare arms boasted the kind of fitness that I admired, but had no desire to obtain. But it wasn't just her appearance that made her pretty, there was something in her presence. A force that drew the eyes and held them. I was, in every way, intimidated.

"Well, the warrior princess rises," the red head said with a roll of her eyes, "well don't just stand there, Kateri, have a seat."

But Kateri was just standing there, she was staring at me. Oh great. What had I done now?

"Your dress is blue," her voice was rich and deep for a woman's, but not unattractive.

I looked down at it. "Yes?" I said, not sure what else I was supposed to say.

"Don't be jealous, Kateri," Rehmea said, lifting a glass in the warrior woman's direction. "Just because Wei couldn't bring himself to love you."

Wait. What? I heard Alan hiss down at the end of the table. If I heard it. Everyone did. What did blue have to do with anything. And, more importantly, what was this about Wei not loving her? I mean, news to me.

"For all your prophecy, it is clear that you know nothing."

Kateri ignored me as she took her own seat. I looked at Vlad, not sure why I was expecting him to explain anything. So far all he had done was watch the melodrama around him with a bemused expression and snap at people who he thought of as servants.

"Blue is the color that only a bride may where when her love has died. When mourning, all where black, except her."

"Wei and I were not married."

He shrugged. "You cared for him. It is obvious."

"It's ridiculous," Kateri said. "There can be no love between that which is vampire and that which is food. A human cannot love a stew."

Well, as someone with a deep and abiding appreciation for food, I wasn't sure that was true, but I wasn't going to say that out loud.

"I love Wei," is what came out of my mouth. I wanted to go on. To tell them that he wasn't dead but a hand wrapped over mine. It was Vlad's.

The tension in the room, already pretty high, radiated. It was a hum in my head. Maybe it was being around all the vampires, but I was getting glimpses of feelings and energies that I just didn't know how to handle. Stupid necromancy, always being confusing. I tried to block it all out, but instead I got little glimpses, images and pictures in my head. Some that made sense, some that didn't.

The first image, I knew, came from Genevieve. It was a repetition in my head of our earlier conversation. More like a gift than an image, a looping repetition of; don't tell him, do not tell him.

She still wasn't telling me why, though.

The next image was, I assume, from Alan. It wasn't a fixed loop like Genevieve's was, but it was of Genevieve. It must have been before she was a vampire. She looked younger, rosy cheeked and jubilant. Her pale hand was patting an older woman's brow. My insight told me that it was her mother, and that she was sick. Then Vlad's hand curled over Genevieve's young shoulder.

It felt creepy.

Then there was Dmitri, big protective lug. He was thinking of charging across the table and slamming his bulk in its hulked-out form, into Vlad. I could feel the desire to do it, to get his father away from me, like a fire simmering in his undead veins.

Then there was Kateri. She was thinking of Wei, of her hands skimming along his chest and going lower. I wasn't sure if it was a memory or a fantasy. Either way it was vivid. I shut it out.

But that left Vlad. And what was happening in his mind involved me and a lot of things that I had only read about.

I jerked my hand away from his, and stepped away from the table so fast that the chair slapped against the floor. I had a deja vu moment of the same thing happening in my own kitchen before I snapped angrily. "What the hell?"

He smiled at me, and it was as sharp as it was silken. "Have I done something to offend?"

I could feel everyone telling me not to do it, not to say it. But let's face it. I'm me. I have the worst habit of doing exactly what people tell me not to do.

"Seriously? Are you kidding? Let's start with the part where you got all kissy with my hand without even asking if I was cool with you touching me. Then how you just watched while your wife beat up on me. I mean, jeez. Here you are, supposed to be this great big commander and Alan, the least violent person I know, is the one who helps me out? What the hell?" I threw my hands up in the air. Rehema was tugging at my sleeve. I ignored her. I had no patience for politeness tonight. I didn't care if Vlad the Impaler decided to flip out on me. I was tired of being scared. "And you know what? That's not even the worst of it, you treat Peter like shit. And you know what? That doesn't fly with me."

"He is a servant."

"Are you serious?" I was so mad I was pretty sure I shrieked it. "Servant doesn't mean less than. I don't know if you know this, but America is all about everyone being equal."

He smiled at me, and it was one of those southern belle smiles. Not pretty and feminine, but the "oh honey" kind of smile. Where you almost feel bad for someone because they've done something stupid. "How young you are to believe such things."

I rolled my eyes. "Don't. Okay? Don't even. I dealt with crappy people all the time when I worked in fast food. They came in there assuming that I was stupid or lazy because of where I worked and treated me and all the people I worked with like crap and then had the audacity to wonder why we weren't super thrilled to take care of them. Nobody is worth more or less than anyone else, but there are a lot of people who think they are."

He continued to look smug. "I have not pleased you with my actions." He stood up, and took my hand in his. The grip was tight enough that I couldn't immediately pull away.

"Yeah. You did."

"Allow me to make recompense. My sons have spoken so well of you, and the prophecy that swims in your veins and I find myself wondering of you."

He said it romantically, as if he was telling me all the beautiful things about me. Again, images of his fangs gliding on my skin entered my head and my body's reaction was to grow tight and tingle. I shivered. It suddenly sounded like an interesting idea.

His lips came to my wrist. It was a pleasant feeling, a good one. No wonder he had so many wives. His lips were like electricity. I remembered Wei's kiss, the feel of his mouth on me and a wave of disquiet pranced along my spine.

"Hey!" I jerked my hand out of his grip and resisted the urge to slap him across the face. "None of those vampire mind tricks on me. I'm like a Troydarian."

"A...what?" He looked at me like I had started speaking a different language. To be fair, I kind of had. If you didn't speak geek you didn't understand the lingo.

"Troydarian, Star Wars. They don't fall for Jedi crap. I'm the necromancer, okay? I know when someone's trying to play with my head. Back off."

His lips formed into an amused line. As previously stated I didn't like it when someone smiled about my anger, especially when that anger was well placed. Dude had tried to use the magical version of a date rape drug. I was beyond pissed.

"Such fire in you."

"My love," Anja said, speaking up for the first time since she had introduced herself. Her voice was a cool wave across the table. "I do not believe that the young lady wishes for your attentions."

He gave her a dubious look, as if he couldn't believe that a woman wouldn't be interested. I wanted to be disgusted by that but if I had three spouses I'd be pretty full of myself too.

"She will learn to be."

"What?" I demanded. My hands were clenching and unclenching at my sides.

He raised his brow. "How else do you plan on fulfilling the prophecy? You need the blood of Vlad, and here I am. Who better to bring magic back into the world than I? I am the beginning of all vampires, all of them are birthed of my blood. The child should be a product of me and my loins."

There it was. The thought I wouldn't even let myself have earlier came to a head. Vlad wanted to be the father of my child. He wanted to be the proud papa with wife number four on his arm, father of magic and keeper of the progeny. And did he seriously just use the word loins?

Ew.

I did what any girl in my position would do. I plucked up my skirts and ran.

CHAPTER FIVE

I made it all the way to the front door before Vlad was in front of me. Damn my human feet and high heeled shoes. He was like some dark shadow standing in front of me, towering and not altogether human. His features were sharper than they had been, more primal. Thanks to Dmitri, and now Yasmina, I knew exactly what was happening. He was shifting shapes. He was gunning for a fight. I came to a halt.

"Move!" I demanded

"Why?" He made the question into something sensual. His teeth were sharp inside of his mouth and the smile he gave me, I think, was supposed to be charming. Near miss.

"Because I want to leave. I thought that was obvious."

"Why?" he asked again. This time the word hissed through inhuman teeth.

"Because you creep me out."

"You have barely grown accustomed to my presence." He stepped forward and reached a hand that was not entirely human out in my direction. I immediately tried to summon my necromantic shield, it didn't work. How nice to have a gift that only popped up when it wanted to. "In time, you would grow to love me."

"It's weird how many guys think that. If a girl just gave them the chance they'd be the perfect boyfriend. Newsflash, Vlad, girls know. I know what I want, and it isn't you."

He sneered at me. "What choice do you have? Your lover is dead and gone."

"No he isn't!" The words were out of my mouth before I could remember that I wasn't supposed to say them. But now that they were I wasn't holding back. "He isn't dead. He's missing. They aren't the same thing."

"What?" It was Alan who spoke. "Wei lives?"

I turned my back on Vlad, showing him just how much he meant to me, and looked at Alan, and the rest of the gathered vampires. Almost all of them were there.

I shrugged. "I mean, as much as any vampire lives, yeah. He's alive. I came over here to tell you that and all I got was..." I waved my hands in a wide circle as if to encompass everything. "So yeah, cat's out of the bag now."

"You lie," Vlad spat. I was surprised that he was angry. Wei was pretty much his kid, right? That's what they kept calling him anyway.

"No." I whirled on him. He looked even less human than he had a moment ago. His features were somewhere between a man, a bat, and a cat. It was pretty in the most terrifying way. "I am not lying. My father has divined that Wei is not dead. He is alive."

"Then, where is he?" Vlad snarled.

"Zane has him."

Okay, that was just an educated guess on my part. I didn't know for sure that Zane had him, or Connie, or my mother. But considering their track record? I would have put a decent amount of money on it.

There was a stirring, and I didn't entirely understand why.

"He...he is alive?" It was Kateri who spoke. She sounded uncertain. I didn't know if she was talking about Wei or Zane. I wasn't sure it mattered.

"Yeah," I said. "He is."

"How do you know this?" Vlad asked.

"My father," I answered. "He divined it."

"A witch's word?" One of the females behind me said, I think it was the Irish one. "How are we to believe that?"

I jerked one shoulder in an angry shrug. "Think what you want. I don't particularly care. You know what? I'm going after him."

I turned and started to move towards the door. If I was going to have to push my way out, so be it. I didn't care. Wei was alive and I had wasted far too much time. It was time to get going.

A hand clapped over my shoulder. Vlad held me in place with all the effort I would have used on a feather. I glared up at him and he looked down at me.

"You say that Zane has him?"

I sighed. "Yeah. Listen. I don't know how close you two are, but Zane and my half-sister have some sort of thing going. I dunno what it is or why or whatever. But my sister believes that the prophecy coming true is a bad thing and I think she has enlisted Zane's help to keep Wei away from me."

He bowed his head. I think he looked sad. I'd feel pity if he hadn't been such a jerk.

"No," he said after a moment.

"No what?" I demanded.

"You will not leave. You will not do this thing."

"Dude, get it through your head. I have no desire to be anywhere near your loins." I poked his chest. I was so beyond caring if it was impolite. "I want one dude, and it is not you."

He sneered at me. "Be that as it may, you cannot go on this quest. I will not allow it."

"Why? Is this some gender thing? Do you think that a woman can't go rescue her man? Because I've got a few thoughts on that."

"No," he said. "It has nothing to do with your gender. It has everything to do with the prophecy."

"Uhh...okay." I tried to jerk my shoulder out of his grip but it was pretty much an exercise in futility. Dmitri was strong, Vlad was stronger. Great.

"Look around you!" he snarled at me. He whirled me around until I looked into the faces of his wives and his children. They stood like some perfect picture of beauty diversified and dressed up in black. Well, everyone but Kateri. "Look at my family, dwindled down to so few. There should be hundreds! Thousands! My children should live in all corners of the world and yet we do not even fill a single dinner table. The loss of one is a madness that none of us can fathom, least of all myself."

I wasn't sure that he hadn't fathomed his own madness, but I wasn't going to say that.

He whirled me around again, taking my face between his hands. The claws pressed into the fullness of my cheeks, hauling me closer. His next words were nearly spoken against my lips.

"I will not let you put yourself in danger. I will not risk the future of my people for you to seek what is already lost."

"I told you already-"

"He. Is. Lost." Vlad enunciated each word carefully. "If what you say is true...he is lost. I will not allow you to do the same."

"Okay, let's get one thing straight." I poked the vampire lord in the chest for the second time, because apparently, I had no fear for my life. "No one, and I seriously mean no one, gets to tell me what I am or am not allowed to do. I grew up barely having a choice in my life, we aren't going to make that a theme in my adult years too."

"Would you doom us all to death?" he asked.

Guilt trip much? I sighed and stepped away. "I get that you are afraid, but I'm not going to let Wei just...go."

"Pity."

I don't know what happened next. But I was looking into those big shadowy eyes of his, my brain got kind of fuzzy, and then next thing I knew I was in a nicely appointed room with absolutely no windows. Oh joy.

CHAPTER SIX

It wasn't the first time that I had been put in a cell designed to look like a room, but I had to admit this one was a lot nicer than the first. There was a four-poster bed, a wide screen television with a PlayStation already hooked up to it, a shelf full of my books as well as books that someone thought that I would like, a quick glance at the titles told me they were probably right. The one and only door that I could find led to a bathroom about half as large as the average bedroom. There was even a mini fridge stocked with a slew of my favorite things to eat.

Well, that did not bode well.

The fact that this single room was stock full of all the necessary amenities that I could need for the next few weeks told me that someone fully expected me to be here for, you know, the next few weeks. I did not have that kind of time. I didn't have any kind of time. I needed to get to Wei.

For about two hours, it was hard to judge because of a serious lack of sunlight, I tried to find a way out. I tested everything that could be a latch, button, or spring for a secret door. I ran my hands over every surface. I even moved the little wingback chair all over so that I could get my hands on the ceiling, you know, just in case. At the end of all that I decided two things. That being short sucked when trying to investigate a room for secret doors, and that whomever had cleaned up this room had done a pretty good job. I was barely dusty.

The room was pretty too, I had to admit. The bed and most of the fabrics were all in shades of pink, the furniture done in light colored woods. It was charming, and bright, despite the lack of light. Well, not a complete lack. There were sconces, and each one with a warm light flickering out.

"Crap," I muttered to myself.

I tugged off the deep blue dress and tossed it on the floor. Normally I wouldn't be so cruel to pretty clothes, but you know what? I was mad and it was literally the only thing to take it out on.

I could guess who tossed me in this room. I knew that Alan and Dmitri wouldn't have dared. Not only because they were my friends, but it would have gone against who they were. Alan might dress up like French Aristocrat, but he was pretty liberal about personal choice and such. Maybe it had something to do with the fact that he had actually grown up under the heel of aristocracy. I didn't know. And Dmitri? A full-blooded Romani? No. He wouldn't. Not even a little. I sighed and flopped onto my unsurprisingly comfortable bed.

The wives? Well, maybe. I didn't know them well enough to say definitively one way or the other, but I got the feeling that they, as well as the daughters, were pretty much pawns of Vlad. Well, maybe pawns wasn't the right word, but they belonged to him in a way that his sons didn't seem to. Maybe I was just reading too much into things. Maybe I was being weird. I didn't know. I just knew that if they had put me here, then it was probably on his orders.

Vlad Tepes, Vlad the Impaler, named for both his father, and the creepy way he had dealt with his enemies. His people had exalted him as a hero who used every ability and skill at his disposal to keep them safe from their enemies. The rest of the world saw him as a monster. I had, until very recently, been willing to give him the benefit of the doubt. Then he had told me he was going to be the father of my prophecy baby and he went fully into monster camp for me. It was my body, my future, and I had a say in how people got to be involved with all that.

I took a deep breath and kicked off the uncomfortable shoes I was still wearing. Genevieve was just a few inches smaller than I was, and her shoes, which had matched the dress perfectly, were equally small. Wearing them had been pretty much torture, but I had been distracted by far more interesting things than my feet. Now it felt like the only thing that I could think of. Maybe my brain just needed something simple to focus on.

A blister. I could handle a blister. I might not be able to figure out how to get out of this stupid room, but I could fix a blister. I rolled off the bed, wandered into the bathroom and ran a bath. A soak. A good, long soak to reset everything and piece together a plan. I could put my pretty epic RPG experience to work and get all of this together.

I spotted my face while the tub was going. I was still wearing all the makeup that Genevieve had put on me. It was pretty, but it didn't suit me at all. For reasons I couldn't even begin to fathom, seeing it all on my face made me mad. I picked up a washcloth and started to scrub, making an absolute mess of her work. When I looked at the leaking eyeliner and smudged lipstick I had to resist an urge to laugh. Then I decided that resisting was stupid and gave in.

The sound of my laughter echoed off the bathroom walls, thrown back at me and letting me know exactly how crazy it sounded. Great, on top of everything else, I was going nuts. I sobered and plopped myself into the bathtub with enough force to have water splashing over the sides.

This had not been my best day. To be honest, it had not been my best month. This month had sucked, in every way possible. Okay, that wasn't true. It wasn't looking up. I hadn't needed to check the entire room to know that I had no way to contact anyone to come and help me. Even if I did, who would I call? My dad? No. I didn't want to bother him, he was working on finding Wei. Jenny would normally have been my first option, but she'd been so scarce. It felt wrong. Everyone else I might have called...well they already knew where I was.

This day had been nothing but ups and downs. One moment I felt like I was the most pathetic creature to ever walk the face of the whole planet. The next I was the most bad ass necromancer to ever summon the undead. It went back and forth, back and forth. I was an emotional yo-yo and it was seriously messing with my head.

I needed to get out of here. There had to be a door. They hadn't built a room around me, so there had to be a way in and out. There was only a couple of weeks' worth of food, so there either had to be a plan to let me go, or bring me more. Maybe, when they did, I could use my necromancy powers to help me get out of the room. Unless Peter was the one bringing me food. Then I'd just ask really nicely. Peter was nice.

So, I guess I had to play the waiting game. Ugh. I was not a fan of the waiting game. Who knew what could be happening to Wei. Who knew what my sister and her vampire boyfriend could be doing to stop the prophecy from happening. Would they hook Wei up to the same blood stealing machines that I had found Zane attached to? I remembered how weak Zane was, how tired. I had trusted him immediately because I thought they had been hurting him. How had he gone back to her after that?

I shook my head. The thoughts were too long and too deep to think about right now. I needed to destress, realign my brain, and get ready. It was video game time. A quick perusal of the dresser offered up some clothing. I found a pair of designer sweatpants, which I hadn't even realized they made, fuzzy socks, and a pale pink t-shirt. Putting the clothes on made me feel better.

As I hadn't gotten dinner and had barely eaten over the past couple of weeks I pulled some food out of the mini fridge, curled up in the wingback chair that I had dragged all over the room, and began to play. I let my brain zone out, got lost in a story, and felt the knots in my neck, back, and shoulders slowly evaporate.

I was so startled when a hand slid over my shoulder that I screamed. I don't scream often, not unless there are roller coasters or spiders involved, but I totally screamed then. I scampered off the chair and along the side of the bed. The popcorn I had been munching flew everywhere.

A man stood at the foot of the bed. It was Vlad, but he didn't look the same as he had at dinner, however long ago that was. His hair had been brushed until it shone in waves around his face. It softened the angles, made him look more approachable. His big dark luminescent eyes looked down at me with charmed amusement. He wore a red robe, and the neckline plunged low enough that I was pretty sure he wasn't wearing much beneath it. Suddenly being on the bed seemed like a bad idea.

I jumped out of it and backed away. I didn't stop until my back met wall.

"What the hell are you doing here?" I demanded, even though it was a stupid question. I had a really good idea what he was doing here. I just didn't want it to be true. "What do you want?"

His smile was slow, seductive, and filled with a charm I hadn't totally expected. He stayed where he was, standing next to the bed. The pale pink sheets didn't look half so sweet with him there.

"I have come to you." He made the words sound rich.

"Nope." It was the first word that came to mind, and the first one that came out of my mouth, but it didn't cover the extent of my feelings. "That's a hard pass. One hundred percent no. Not gonna happen."

He reached a hand out to me. He did it slowly, with the kind of elegant muscle control that a human just didn't have. I could watch every single movement of muscle. It was strangely hypnotic. The fingers were long and pale, and the unfolded like a fan towards me. The tips of them decorated with nails long and sharp enough that I knew that they could cut. He turned the palm over, offering it to me. I glared.

"Does the word no mean nothing to you?"

His smile was nothing but charm. I could hear the laughter in his words when he said, "it is not a word I hear often."

"Yeah, I bet when you surround yourself with nothing but simpering brides and doting daughters it isn't." I rolled my eyes. "Sorry, I'm not interested in a dude who can't take criticism."

He laughed, and it was so rich and warm that I felt it dance over my skin. "It has been a long time since a woman has turned me down so genuinely. I find it intoxicating."

I made a face. "Are you serious? That's...okay that's like really gross. Hearing a girl tell you no is a turn on? What kind of creep are you? Wait." I held up a finger. "You know what? Don't tell me. I don't need to know. You are creepy. I got it."

He frowned now, and he didn't look half so charming. "You do not find me intriguing?"

I tried my best not to laugh. He was being absolutely serious. "Dude, some chicks go for that over assertive, alpha male "you know you want me" thing. That's their choice. Me? I'm not big on overconfidence. And all this." I waved a hand up and down to encompass his body. "This is nothing but overconfidence."

His face went carefully blank. It reminded me a little of Alan when he was trying to hide something. I think I had offended him. "I wish to seduce you."

I did my best not to roll my eyes, but it took everything in me not to. "You made that absolutely clear. To be honest you came on a little strong when you announced to an entire table of your sons, daughters, and wives that that was your intent. And you did it at the supposed funeral dinner of the guy I love."

"It bothers you that I am honest with them?" He withdrew his hand as slowly as he had extended it, and despite the fact that I was boiling with anger it was still interesting to watch.

Okay, this time I totally rolled my eyes. "Honesty is fantastic, revealing private information? That's just crappy."

"You believe seduction should be a private matter."

I dragged a hand down my face. It was like I was trying to train a puppy. A tall, undead, thousand-year-old puppy. "That is just the tip of the iceberg here, but yes. Seduction should be a private matter. But you are missing the point. I don't want you to seduce me."

He eyed me, clearly not understanding my issues here. "I am very pleasant company."

"Dude, you have greatly overestimated your charms."

"Do you not want me?"

"No," I said as flatly as I could. "I don't. I'm sorry. I don't have time for the gentle let-down here. But I'm just not interested."

He frowned at me. "I have never had a woman so determinedly say no."

I shrugged, feeling very little in the way of pity. "Welcome to the new era of the modern woman. We don't say maybe when we mean no. At least I don't. I love Wei. I am sorry that doesn't compute in your grand scheme of things. But I am not interested in you."

His lip curled into a sneer. One minute he was at the edge of my bed, watching me the way a cat watches a bird, and the next he was in front of me. Vampires moved fast, all of them, but he seemed to teleport. I felt the prick of his nails against my skin as he took my chin in his hand.

"But I am interested in you." His eyes seemed to burn into me. I could feel magic, hot and heavy pounding down on me. It took me a moment to understand that he was laying the creepy magics down and trying to make me feel how much he wanted me. Ew.

If I had been someone else, anyone else, I might have fallen victim to that hypnotic gaze of his. But I was a necromancer, and their mind tricks, even those of Vlad himself, just didn't work on me. I screwed up my face to show how much I wasn't interested. "Tough."

I think he finally got it. His hand squeezed and I felt the bones in my jaw creak. It vibrated strangely in my ears. "I do not think you fully understand the depth of your position. My life depends on the creature you spawn. This can be gentle, a mutual pleasure, or not. I leave the choice in your hands."

Anger surged around me. I knew exactly what he was threatening and I was not cool with it. I opened myself up to my magic in a way I don't think I ever had before. It was, as it had always been, like a door opening in my mind, but more organic than that. It was my mind opening, my spirit, my soul. It wasn't just a part of me the way my hair was, or even my eye color, or my skin. Those things fell out, got scrubbed off, or changed with time. This was something else. Something deep inside that was as much a part of me as my love of comic books and the pride I had at getting through the boss level in that vampire game I like. It was my love of broken-in boots and jeans that fit just right. This was me in the way that time couldn't change.

I was a Necromancer and he was a vampire.

I slapped him. I slapped him hard. It had all the effect of hitting a marble statue. Pain radiated from my palm to my wrist and up. But I didn't care. He had crossed that line between threats that made me roll my eyes and threats that made me mad. He gave me a smile, amused by my attempt at hitting him, and then the magic flowed down my arm, pushing back the pain. It was a chaotic burst of arcane power, that slammed into him like a fist. His head jerked suddenly to the side and he flew back several inches.

"Back. Off." I snapped.

When he looked at me, the beauty of his face had disappeared. His teeth were long and sharp in his mouth. The skin stretched over his forehead until it was more like a saphead. I could see the veins standing out beneath his skin like a tapestry. It wasn't pretty, not like it was with Anja. He hissed at me. I wrapped my magic around me like a glove.

"This is my choice to make." My voice reverberated through the room with power. "Not yours. You cannot, you will not touch me."

He lunged at me and I threw my hands out. A shield wove around me, invisible but tangible. He slammed against it impotently. I felt his power though. It was, I hated to admit, impressive. He was the first of his kind.

"You will be mine."

"The hell I will."

He slammed again. The Shield held, but I wasn't sure that it would forever. It didn't crack. It wasn't glass, but it seemed to vibrate around me, and when it went steady again it wasn't half so powerful feeling.

"I will not die for your prudish morality."

I laughed bitterly. "If you think that's the problem, you are out of touch. Let me out of here. Let me go find Wei."

He sneered, and dragged one clawed finger down my shield. It didn't make a sound, but a sensation. As if I were the chalkboard and him the nail. I could feel it in my teeth. "You would go to him when you could have me."

"Duh."

He withdrew his hand, and his face slowly turned back into the vampire that I was a little more familiar with. "He is dead."

I shook my head once. "No, he isn't."

His eyes bore into mine. "You love him?"

It was a question, so I answered it. "Yes."

"And you believe he loves you."

This was more like a statement, but I answered it anyway. "Yes."

He sighed, and this time he looked at me with pity. "I have known Wei for a thousand years. I have never known a more stubborn and determined person in all of my time walking this grand earth. If the love between you is true...as you so obviously believe, he would not be away from you now. He would have removed his own foot to be back at your side. Not even Zane could stop him."

And then he turned to smoke and vanished. I hadn't known that a vampire could do that. I'd never seen it before, but there he went. But that wasn't what had me sliding down the wall.

Was he right? I knew Wei too, and stubborn was definitely a word I associated with him. Determined, well, yes...he was that too. Was Vlad, who had known him literally a thousand times longer than I had, right? Maybe Wei didn't love me. Just because I cared about him didn't mean he cared about me.

The desire to curl back up on the bed and forget about the world began to sink down around me.

I shook my head. No, I had felt it. I had literally felt his love for me. It felt like years ago, but it wasn't. A month? Six weeks? Not even. I shook my head and gave up trying to figure out the timeline of my own life and focused on what had mattered. Wei loved me, and he had loved me before I had loved him.

I had to get out of here. For the second time, I started pushing every spot on the walls, trying to find some kind of secret button. Not even a smidgen of luck. Everything felt so wrong, so desperately wrong. Tears threatened to spring out of my eyes and that just made me so mad. I was done with crying. I had been crying too much and I totally did not want that. I got mad, and, for lack of a better term, I flipped out.

I hated that everything around me looked so nice and neat when I felt so wrong, so I just started breaking stuff. Some stuff I broke with my hands, some with magic. I can't remember it clearly. It was almost like I was watching myself go nuts rather than being inside of my body. I broke the television, the bookshelf, I threw books across the room and I kicked the mattress off the bed.

This was a jail, no matter how pretty, and no one was coming to rescue me. I was angry, I was hurt, and when I finally came down off that mad angry high I was exhausted. I curled up in a pile of sheets and fell asleep against the mattress, rather than on it.

I had no idea how long passed. When I woke up I grabbed a yogurt and a bottle of water from the fridge, ate both, didn't bother throwing anything away. I read a book that hadn't been destroyed, made a sandwich, drank more water and went back to sleep. Without the sun or a video game that tracked my played hours, or even a television, I had no idea how much time passed. It just did. My life, for who knew how long, became a cycle of wake up, eat, distract myself, and go back to sleep.

Vlad visited again, it went about as well as the first time with a few scathing remarks about how good of a housewife I was. I made a rude gesture in response because I didn't really see a reason to oblige his sexism with words. He was still certain that he would make the best father for my child, but he wasn't stupid enough to try to attack me again. And when I had tried to attack him he did that vanishing act on me.

I did, however, realize that he wasn't getting into my room through a door, exactly. He was turning into mist and going through walls. Neat trick. But it wasn't going to help me. And on the third visit, when he managed to bring food with him through the mist, I realized that I wasn't going to get out as I had originally planned.

You can bet there was another angry rampage happening after that. I yelled and I screamed and I threw things. And then I got mad at myself for going crazy. Weird, right? I looked down at myself, holding the dwindling bottle of expensive shampoo that I had been intent on throwing and realized that this kind of anger? It wasn't the productive kind. It was impotent and pitiful and I was tired of being those two things. I needed a new plan, and I needed it now.

When I turned back to the bed Maahes was there.

"Well hello there, you useless feline," I said with as much affection as I could manage, given that I was shaking. I plopped down on the chair, and he joined me a moment later. His weight was comforting. I began to pet my fingers through his ghostly fur. "What is with people wanting to trap me?" I asked, not expecting an answer. He rolled over and stretched, offering up the super soft belly.

I sat there for a long moment, trying to come up with a plan that didn't involve me digging beneath the house.

"I need to get out of here, Maahes," I said absently. "I need to get out and get all of this...done."

Maahes stretched out and hopped off of my lap. I thought that he was abandoning me until he started to sniff around different corners of the room. And then, in the way of a ghost cat, his slender body pushed through a wall.

"Maahes?" I asked, knowing I sounded pathetic. Sure, I was surrounded by a junk food dream and had books and video games aplenty, but I seriously did not want to be alone again.

Then as if by magic, a part of the wall pushed open. Maahes stood there, looking up at me expectantly.

"Holy crap, what did you just do?" I asked the cat.

He continued to sit there, looking up at me with feline bemusement. I jumped up from the bed and nearly scampered over to the newly revealed door. It was deeper than I thought. Also, it was merely one of a pair of doors. There were two doors, with about a foot of space between them. There was a switch on either side. Someone would have to be a vampire who could do the smoke thing, or a ghost, to get to them.

I flipped the switch closer to the other door and it swung open to reveal a hallway that was alien and familiar all at once. I knew by the structure and styling that it was a part of the mansion, but it was somewhere I had never been before. The walls, the same wood as everywhere else, were bare of Dmitri's art, or Alan's elegant touches, or even Wei's carpentry.

"Alright Maahes," I said softly, as if afraid someone was going to hear me, "lead the way."

He did. I wasn't sure if I was amused or surprised or a little of both. The cat tail curled high into the air in the shape of a question mark and Maahes trotted down the long hallway, leading me out.

If it sounds like I was cucumber calm, I wasn't. My heart was pounding so hard that I was pretty sure I could see my pulse going through my eyes. I was happy I was wearing socks, not shoes. My feet made almost no sound as I slunk from one end of the hallway to the other, looking for a way out.

The last time that I had to break out of anywhere I'd had a friend, or at least an accomplice. This time it was just me and my ghost cat trying not to make any noise. Okay, I was the one trying not to make any noise. Maahes did not have that problem. Ghost feet didn't make much sound. Not even when we finally made our way into familiar territory.

Everything was exactly as I remembered it and different all at the same time. I still had no idea how long I had been trapped in that room, but it was long enough that the mansion had been redecorated.

The warmth of Dmitri's artwork had been replaced by those antique portrait paintings that you see in old castles. Most of them were of him. Some showed him on horseback, some in armor, some on thrones. The clothes changed with the times, he didn't. The others were of his wives and daughters. Most were classy, and a pretty significant amount were naked. Even his daughters. Gross.

There were absolutely no pictures of Wei, or any of the sons. That sparked a sick feeling in my stomach. Or maybe that was the adrenaline mixing with the fact that I hadn't had what you might call a proper meal in what felt like forever.

I ignored it, and tried to ignore the fact that it wasn't just the pictures that were missing. The charming touches of Alan's decorating skills were just as absent, leaving the mansion feeling cold.

Out of instinct I made my way towards the kitchen. I had spent a lot of time there when I had been living in the house. Not just because I was human, but because food was pretty much the best thing ever. As I approached I heard noises.

"This is the menu for tonight," a female voice was saying. I think it was Anja. "He wishes for dinner to be served promptly at three in the morning."

"Yes, ma'am." I instantly recognized Peter.

There was a long silence. "Is there a problem?"

"The amounts seem to be short."

"No, this is all the master and us require."

Another long pause. "Master Alan and Master Dmitri will not be attending dinner...again?"

The sound of skin striking skin echoed through the door. "A servant does not speak of dinner guests, he is required only to carry out his duties. If you cannot do that, you will be...dealt with. Is that understood?"

"Yes...ma'am."

I ducked down and slunk around the long fancy island when I heard the door open. When I saw Anja's full skirts rustle by I had to resist the urge to attack her. I didn't like her hitting Peter. To be honest, I wasn't cool with hitting someone in the first place. I know that they say video games are supposed to make you violent, but I find killing my digital enemies soothing. My real ones? Well that takes a toll.

When I was sure she was gone I went from the kitchen to the pantry where I found Peter, hunched over what looked like an industrial sized thing of water ketchup. One sniff told me that it was definitely blood. Ew. He was leaning over it, his head pressed against an empty shelf. His shoulders slumped forward.

"Peter?"

He jerked up, his eyes wide with fright. "I wasn't dawdling!" he cried out.

I had never seen Peter look anything but perfectly pressed and polished. Yes, he had smiled, laughed, and joked with the Sons of Vlad, but he had never seemed afraid. The wide-eyed stare he was giving me, and the shaking of his hand as he fidgeted with the big bucket of blood made me think that he was well beyond scared and deeply afraid.

"Peter," I said again, softly this time. "Are you okay?"

He blinked, his eyes softening for just a moment. "Lorena?"

"That's me," I said, stepping forward and putting my hand on his shoulder. "Are you alright? Where are Alan and Dmitri? What's going on?"

He started to shake again, and I tugged him away from the pantry. I didn't know how safe the kitchen was, so I pulled him deeper into the servants' area. I was pretty sure none of the high and mighty vampires would come this way. Eventually we ended up in a room that looked like Peter's private quarters. He sat on a love seat, still looking at me like I was a ghost.

"Lorena, you are here. I thought...they had put you away."

"They had," I admitted. "But being a necromancer pretty much rocks. But how long was I gone?"

"A week," he said.

I wasn't sure how I felt about that. There was a part of me that feel like I had been in that crappy room for months, and another part that wondered if it had only been a day or two. A week? That was...well that wasn't the worst news that I could have gotten.

"Alright," I said. "Tell me everything."

He did. I had to make him a cup of tea to help him stop shaking, but ultimately, he told me the story of Vlad's budding reign of terror. It had started when he had demanded that everyone forget that Wei was alive. I didn't get that. I mean, I knew that he thought that if I believed Wei was dead it would mean I'd jump into Vlad's arms...but what did it matter if everyone else thought he was alive? I didn't know, but when Alan and Dmitri refused he had them locked up too. Apparently, Vlad believed that locking people up and refusing them sustenance meant that they'd learn respect. Yeah, fear and respect weren't the same thing. Whatever.

Then Vlad had decided to redecorate. Instead of going back to Transylvania or wherever, he had decided that this new and lush world was the new home for him and his people. It was where they would make their army.

"What army?" I asked.

"Vlad has...lost the ability to create more vampires." Peter's voice was conspiratorially low. I had to lean in to hear him. I had already known that, but it was clear that Peter didn't think I had. "He thinks once he gets you pregnant that he will be able to make more, and when he does he wants to make hundreds, thousands."

"Why?"

"To rule the world," a light feminine voice said.

I jumped, so did Peter. I whirled and found myself looking into the perfect face of Genevieve. Her dress was the palest rose petal pink I had ever seen, but it wasn't as fancy as the other gowns I knew she owned. It had the straighter lines of a riding gown.

She held up a single hand. "I am not here to harm you. I am here to assist."

"Assist?" I asked, knowing I sounded disbelieving.

She sighed. "I want magic back in this world, Lorena Quinn. I will not lie about that. I will, however, say that the idea of Vlad fathering that magic makes the blood grow cold in my belly. I do not know if it is the loss of magic, or the believed loss of two of his sons, and he does believe them lost. But he has gone mad. Every night it is worse. I have heard him whisper your name when he comes to one of our beds. I have heard him walk the length of your hallway and wonder why you do not submit to his charms. Lorena, I fear for you, myself, and my brother."

I believed her. Maybe it was stupid, but I did. "What can you do?"

"I can get you out of here."

"What of Alan? Dmitri? Peter?"

"I cannot free them. Not without him knowing. And if he knew that you were helped in the escape...not all of us would survive the aftermath."

"I'll stay," Peter said bravely. "He needs his comforts. I will provide them."

I shook my head. "I can't leave Alan and Dmitri locked away." I shook my head a second time, harder. All I could picture was them in a room, unable to leave, while the days crawled by. No, I wouldn't leave anyone that way, not even someone I hated. "I can't leave you two to fight this battle without me."

"We aren't," Genevieve promised. "Not all of the vampires agree with Vlad and what he is doing. Anja does, because she is dedicated to him in a way that only his first bride can be, and Rehma is his favorite, and she won't do anything to risk that changing. But the rest of us? Well." She shrugged a pale shoulder and looked amused with herself. "I am very charming."

I didn't know exactly what she meant by that. But I didn't need to. "You'll make sure that Alan and Dmitri are safe?"

"I will make sure no harm comes to my brother or his love." Genevieve smiled. "You must go. You must rescue Wei." She reached out and took my hand in hers. "Please, Lorena, rescue your heart so that we do not all lose."

CHAPTER SEVEN

After so long of nothing happening, everything went quickly after that. I had so many questions I wanted to ask, but before I could even form the words, I was given new clothes and shown out the servants' door to disappear into the night in record time. I was promised that everything at the mansion would be taken care of, and I had to trust in that.

The keys to a car that wasn't mine jingled in my hand. When I saw what they went to, I nearly froze. I was expecting one of the dark SUV's that I had seen the vampires drive when they had bothered to drive rather than use their fancy magical transportation abilities. This? This was the kind of car you'd see in a slick action movie. It had the Pontiac symbol on the front, but I didn't know what fancy title they had given this curvy and sleek car.

"Holy..." I shook my head and smirked.

I jumped in the car, and a moment later Maahes appeared in the passenger's seat. "Hey buddy, thanks for the great escape.

His response was to sniff the leather. I couldn't blame him. The leather was nice. So were all the pretty display options on the dashboard. No expense was spared with this car was concerned. I approved.

I put the key in the ignition and took off into the night. I didn't bother with AC, I rolled the power windows down and let the fresh air tangle my hair. It cleared my head long enough for me to make a plan.

I was going to stop by the house first and let my dad know I wasn't dead. While I was there I was going to load up on all the magical crap my grandmother had laying around, arming myself like Rambo did with guns. Then I was going to pick up a burner phone so I could stay in contact with people. Then I was going to Jenny's. I didn't care how happy her life was without me in it, I had a few things to say about being abandoned. I hadn't had a whole lot of friends in my life, but I knew that you weren't supposed to ignore them just because you got a love interest. That just wasn't cool.

Then, when all that was done, I was going to go find Wei. Either he was at the creepy cult compound, or someone there knew where he was. One way or another I was going to find out where he was.

There was a light on at the house as I pulled into the driveway. Before I even got out of the fancy, fancy, car the door was opening and the familiar shape of my father filled the light that came spilling out.

"Lorena?" he asked, and I heard his voice break.

"The one and only."

Before I could make some smart quip, he was wrapping me in his arms and holding me so tight breathing became an option. I couldn't blame him, but it was the first time I really remember him really hugging me. Sure, he'd hugged me on my birthday or when I wasn't feeling well. This was different. He'd thought I was gone forever and I could feel it. I felt bad, but more than that, I was angry at Vlad for making me worry my father. "Where were you? What happened?"

"Let's talk inside." I felt strangely exposed standing outside of the house, my house. I had to keep reminding myself that it was mine. Stupid, but true.

He didn't let go of me, he loosened his grip and lead me inside, but he kept an arm slung around me as if he were afraid I was going to disappear. I couldn't blame him. Over a cup of hot chocolate, I told him everything, from the dinner to Vlad to the great escape. Then I asked him if he'd figured out the math magic thing.

"You want to talk about that right now?" he asked. There was something in the way that he said it that had me looking him over. My dad looked tired. Not just kind of sleepy, like my arrival had woken him up, but really tired. The kind of tired that a whole month of sleep couldn't fix. His brown hair looked a little more silver than I remembered it and there were bags under his eyes. He wore jeans and a t-shirt and no socks to speak of.

I shrugged. "Well, I don't plan on sleeping for a week since that's pretty much all I've done. So, let's talk about this."

He dragged a hand down his face and then stood up. He went to one of the magic book shelves and took out what looked to be a fancy leather notebook. He opened it up and I realized it was filled with equations. The Mathmagician's grimoire, I supposed.

"Okay," he said, plopping the book down in front of me. "I have done a little over one hundred equations and what I've discovered is that Wei is at the compound for the Order of the Loyal Hermit, and that he is neither alive nor dead. I don't know how that is, or why that is."

The first part came as absolutely no surprise, the second one? Well that was a whole different thing. "Because he's a vampire?" I guessed.

He shook his head. "Vampires have their own numbers, like shape shifters and other mythical beings. Some of those numbers overlap, but that's not the reason for this. I don't know what's going on, but he exists in some in-between state that I can't get an equation for."

"Okay, that took a hundred equations?"

He frowned deep enough to cause lines around his eyes and shook his head. "No, the rest came when I was trying to find out if you were with Jenny or the vampires."

"Well, I hope that question got answered."

"It did...and it didn't."

I didn't like the way that sounded. My life these past few months (was it really only months?) had been one problem after another and

I had the distinct feeling that I was about to have another one handed to me. "You wanna make that a little less vague for me, pops?"

He gave me a look that told me he was about as amused with me as he would be with a fungal infection. "You should focus."

"I am focused. Right now, I am focused on the fact that you don't want to tell me what's going on with Jenny." I gave him my own look, but I didn't think it was nearly as polished.

"I can't explain what I found, but I think that something is wrong where Jenny is concerned," he finally said after our battle of the expressions. "Maybe Reikah too, I can't be sure." He didn't look at me when he said it.

Despite the fact that I wasn't too happy with her right this moment, I felt a little flip happen in my belly. I could taste guilt in the back of my throat like old sour fruit. "What do you mean? Like, you mean they might be having trouble in paradise problems? Or like, cult apocalypse problems?"

"I don't know." He jerked his shoulders nearly up to his ears. The new lines around his eyes looked deeper than they had at first. He wasn't just tired, he was scared. I don't know that I had ever seen my dad scared before. I picked up my keys. "Where are you going?" His head snapped up as he came to attention.

"My list of people to rescue just got a little longer." I tucked the keys into my pocket and turned towards my grandmother's shelves. "It's time to load up and roll out. Are you coming?"

My father paused, he ran his tongue along his teeth. "Lorena, my magic is passive, not active. I need time to craft equations, to select the right numbers, use the right paper and ink to create the frame for my spell work. Informative, but not particularly good in any combat situation." He dragged his hand through his hair again, several locks stuck up. "For a long, long time no one thought that I had any magic because it takes such a specific set of circumstances for me to spell work."

There was a flicker of something behind his eyes that told me this had been a sore point. As much as I wanted to reminisce over my father's childhood trauma I couldn't right this moment. Maybe another time.

"Okay, so you are the font of wisdom back at home base," I said, putting my RPG knowledge to work. "At least you aren't an annoying fairy that follows me around."

"What?"

"Zelda joke. Don't worry about it. But I have to go. I have to go see what's happening with Jenny, I have to go find out what's going on with Wei, and then I have to see if I can fulfill a prophecy without one side trying to kill me and the other side trying to...attack me." I couldn't bring myself to say the type of attack. It still made my skin crawl.

"What do you need from me?"

I began going through the crystals and glass bottles filled with dried herbs on the bookshelf. I didn't know the properties of all of them, or even half, but I knew enough to know what might help focus my magic. "Can you cast magic on me? I dunno, write your mathematical symbols on me or something? Protective ones, you know, or anything that can elevate my magic?"

I had the feeling I was going to need my magic, and a lot of it. I just wish I knew what for. I wish that I knew better how to handle my magic. That I had more time, or some kind of wise witch to give me all the information right before I went to the boss battle. Apparently, life was not that straight forward.

"I can give you three things," he said, sounding more and more like a quest giver. That was about right, considering I was on a quest. "I can give you a map of the compound, I am sure it hasn't changed much since your mother and I were...together."

"You spent time there?"

He sighed. "I had a rebellious time, it took a few equations to get that. Some protections, and..." he hesitated. "The wand."

That had me pausing with a crystal in my hand. "The what?"

He turned away from me, and reached into the high cabinet nestled over the fridge. He pushed past the flour and brown sugar containers and pulled out what looked like a tall canister marked Pasta. He lifted the lid and pulled out a very simple slip of wood, no longer than the span between my wrist and my elbow and no wider around than my thumb. It was incredibly simple to look at, just smooth honey colored wood with a smooth white crystal affixed to the end.

"Your grandmother's wand. I should have given it to you before, but I thought...well I guess I was still protecting you."

I felt a small tinge of anger, but it was drowned out by the fact that I could almost feel magic spilling off the wand. It felt like an invisible cloud sweeping through me.

"Will it work for me?" I asked.

He nodded. "It should."

He put it in my hand and a tingle slithered up my arm. It didn't feel bad or scary or anything, it felt good.

"Is there a pointy hat hiding behind the sugar or something?"

My dad laughed. "No. But there are some robes."

When I got into the car twenty minutes later I was wearing a set of dark green robes with silver symbols around the edges. The symbols, according to my dad, were protective in nature, and would help me better than any armor. I believed him, but I paired the robes with a pair of batman leggings and boots anyway. Apparently, I was about six inches taller than my grandmother had been.

I had a belt too, with a bunch of pouches. They weren't leather, like you might see in some cheesy fantasy film, they were made of floral print fabrics, like you'd get at a sewing shop. Each one was filled with what could only be called witchcraft supplies. Crystals in one, little bottles of herbs in another, and a bunch of salt in the last. I probably should have spent more time researching what works best for a necromancer, but I was going to have to work with what I had.

When I took the wheel in my hands the sleeves of my robe slithered up a few inches to show off the mathematical symbols that made spiraling bracelets up my arms. I didn't understand them, but Dad swore they would help me. I was just going to have to accept that.

"You stay safe," I told Dad, rolling down the window. I could see the concern knitting his brows together and I almost felt guilty that he couldn't come.

"Between the two of us, I think that you are the one who is going to be in more danger."

He wasn't wrong. But I put the car into gear and sped out of the driveway anyway.

～～

I knew something was wrong the moment I drove by the mini-mart. It was a little twenty-four-hour gas station that Marquessa Green, Jenny's grandmother, owned. She had left it in Jenny's seemingly capable hands. Every time I had ever gone by the big sign over the door had said OPEN. Now? It looked pretty much abandoned. It wasn't just that it was closed, it was the stack of bills tucked into the slot, and the pile of newspapers making a small mountain outside the front door. As I watched. a guy in a pickup truck approached, and despite overwhelming evidence to the contrary, tried to open the front door. It didn't budge.

That was definitely weird.

I'd only been to Jenny's house once, but I found my way there as if I had been a million times. There weren't a lot of houses in this two-stop-light town. The mountains made it hard, and I suspected the vampires, who owned pretty much everything around here, didn't lease a lot of land for development. I drove towards the simple one level ranch style home and was surprised to see twenty or so cars parked up and down the street. There weren't that many houses, a lot of the space was taken up by a really old church. I had to drive all the way down the street to find a place to park.

My skin started to itch with the knowledge that something was wrong. It wasn't any kind of magic, just the sort of thing you know when everything else in your life had gone wrong.

I parked the car and got out, regretting it nearly the moment I did.

Jenny's house was located on a little stretch of road called Hunter's Lane. It was just over two football fields long, with six houses sprinkled up one side and down the other. They didn't match, the way you'd find in suburban housing development, but they all shared that lived in look that you got in places older than forty years. There were no fences, accept small ones around gardens, and it was easy to see that the only house where anything was happening was Jenny's.

All the other houses were empty. The lights were off, the driveways were empty, and mailboxes had been left open. One yard was a murky flooded wasteland where someone had left a hose half turned on. Another door was left open, a yawning square of black against a mint green trim as if clearly stating that no one was home. On top of all that, there were no animals. No dogs wandering down the abandoned street, no tell-tale signs of glittering cat eyes. In fact, aside from the yellow gleam of lights coming from Jenny's house, there was absolutely nothing happening.

That was...weird.

Maahes appeared next to me, his ghostly tail wrapping around my ankle as if he wasn't any happier to be here than I was. I knelt down, gave the space between his ears a gentle rub, not sure if I was comforting myself and the skipping heartbeat in my chest, or the spectral cat.

"Alright, let's go scooby-doo on this."

I reached inside my robes and pulled out the wand. It nearly jumped into my hand. Its light weight was a comfort in my palm.

"Rescue Jenny, rescue Wei, fulfill prophecy...dragons." I reminded myself of my goals before taking the long walk down the deserted street. I mean, if a best friend, a hot dude, and mythical fire breathing flying beasts weren't enough to inspire me then what was?

A mist rose up around my ankles, nearly rendering Maahes invisible as old road in desperate need of repair crunched beneath my boots. It wasn't a usual mist, the kind you might get if you lived in the valley. This was too dense, and too high up the mountain this time of year. Also, it smelled kinda like old gym socks and wet dog, two of my least favorite smells.

The door was half open when I approached. The mist was coming out of it, like it was a fridge door left open. I put my hand on it and pushed and it took a little too much strength to get it to move. The scent was nauseating as I stepped over the threshold. Maahes lingered on the porch.

"Scaredy-cat."

He wasn't amused. There was a pretty big part of me that wanted to linger just inside the door and trade witty repartee with my cat, but that wasn't particularly heroic. I took a deep breath, asked myself what would Wonder Woman do, and then headed into the living room.

Marquessa Green was a clean woman. She wasn't obsessively neat, the way some people could be, but she liked things in their place. The living room that stretched out before me was not Marquessa Green's, and I seriously mean stretched. The room looked to be fifty yards long, and I knew that wasn't right. The proportions pretty much everywhere were screwy. The family pictures on the wall were too thin and too long. The sofa looked like it could fit have of the Justice League and their comic book sized egos. Everything was wrong, and everything was covered in mist.

Despite the incredible amount of cars the entire living room was empty. It was just a long deep brown couch stretched along an impossibly lengthy wall. I checked the kitchen, which was equally disproportionate, and there was nothing there either, just the remnants of a dinner that looked several weeks too old to be good. A lone fly made lazy circles over the top of a chicken carcass. I could smell the tinge of rot mingling with the other smells and I had to leave before I got sick everywhere. I hadn't had nearly enough to eat to throw it up.

Where was everyone?

In the end, I followed the mist. It had to be coming from some central point, right? So I put my arm across my mouth in the hopes of blocking out all the smell. It wasn't until I got through the kitchen that I spotted something that should not be there.

The Green house was a single-story ranch, there were no stairs, yet there was a set, , made of wood and wrought iron. They spiraled up to a second story that I knew did not exist.

"Well, I guess that answers that," I grumbled to myself.

I did not want to go up those stairs, but heroes didn't have a choice. Okay, that's not true. I could have just said that this was too much for me, that I needed to leave and go one level up and go somewhere before coming back. If this had been a video game that's pretty much exactly what I would have done. But my friend, my one and only friend, and her girlfriend might not be okay. I had to do something about that. I should have done something about this weeks ago but I had been so wrapped up in my own issues that I hadn't even thought anything of Jenny's sudden absence.

I made my way up the staircase. The mist was cold around my ankles, and the stairs creaked under my boots. It was way colder upstairs than it had been downstairs. I could see my breath by the time I got to the very top. It came out in short puffs as I looked from one side to the other.

There was a hall, as unbelievably long as the house downstairs had been. It reminded me a little of the hallways at the mansion, but there was nothing elegant about this. This had the cold lines and colder colors of a hospital wing. There were twenty doors, unevenly spread out on either side of the hall. The floors were white. At least I thought they were white. The mist was getting hard to see through.

I stood there and listened for a moment, hoping that some sound would guide me to where I needed to go. I really did not want to play "What's behind door number 1?" in this weird place. I didn't hear anything, just the soft rustle of my own robes as I breathed.

"Any ideas, Maahes?"

The ghost cat wrapped his tail around my ankle, assuring me of his presence, but offered nothing else.

"Guessing games it is."

As I approached the front door I noticed that there was a name plaque across the center of it, just around eye level. There wasn't a name on it, though, there was a circle of runes. Runes, I frowned, I knew those. I wasn't an expert or anything, but Reikah had taught me the basics. Runes, and similar symbols were a part of the Hermit's magical background. Since they believed in all witches being taught the exact same stuff, in law and order and all that crap, they used the same symbols.

I looked the symbols over. I knew that they were binding symbols, meant to either keep something out, or something in. Maybe both. Like I said, I was in no way an expert. There was also the symbol for witch or heretic, when it came to the Order those two were pretty much interchangeable.

Well, I was looking for a witch. With a deep breath, I put my hand on the door and pushed. It pushed back. Not with force but with magic. The moment my hand hit the handle it warmed, and then it grew hot. Instinct took over and I jerked my hand away from the knob and then I went flying across the short hallway, my back slamming into the wall behind me.

The air left my lungs in a whoosh and I was pretty sure I saw cartoon stars around my eyes.

That was...different. I had been on the receiving end of magic before, but nothing quite like that. My entire arm was tingling and my head was spinning. I held up my arm and saw the magical numbers scrawled over my skin were sparkling. It was hard to draw a breath. *Crap.* I could only imagine what might have happened to me if I hadn't let go of the doorknob. From the tingling in my arm I could only assume something terrible.

"Thanks, Dad," I muttered to myself. He totally would have been helpful here. I brushed my hands off on my robes and stood up. "Okay, Lorena. Think."

I knew some magical circle magic. I needed to put that to use. I also knew a little bit about symbology. I needed that too. I just needed to be careful. I took a breath and stood up.

Touching the door was a no-no. I could persuade Maahes to go into the rooms, but what good would that do? He couldn't tell me what was going on inside of there, and he couldn't bring whatever was in there out. Too bad the house wasn't haunted, that would have worked in my favor.

Wait. There was a church. Churches had graveyards, and graveyards had ghosts. I'd never tried summoning a ghost before, but I'd called to vampires. This couldn't be all that different, right? I reached into one of the pouches and pulled out a crystal. It was smooth and dark and cool to the touch.

I hadn't done a lot of work with crystals or stones. Some, yes, but not a lot. In retrospect, I should have spent more time practicing. Oh well.

I sat on the ground, the mist swimming up over my thighs. A moment later the weight of a cat slithered into my lap and I gave Maahes a pet. Him being there settled my nerves. I took a breath and closed my eyes.

If I had been a mage this might not have worked. Mages were big into planning, into the creation of circles, and ritualistic spell casting. For a mage, or a wizard depending on what they wanted to be called, planning was everything. As a full-fledged witch, I might not have been able to do this either. Half of a witch's power was in being absolutely certain in herself, and I was in no way, shape, or form certain in what I was about to do. Thanks to Reikah and Jenny I had a little bit of training in both. I hoped it would be enough.

I closed my eyes, stilled my mind, and focused on the weight of the crystal in my hand. It was warmer now than it had been, and holding it eased the lingering pain in my arm.

Meditation wasn't really about clearing the mind, it was more about organizing it. Sorta like cleaning up my room. I didn't throw everything out, I just put things where they were supposed to go. I couldn't worry about Jenny or Reikah or Wei. That was for another time. Right now, I needed to access that part of me that called to the dead, in the hopes of calling the dead to me. I focused on the stone. I ran my thumb across the top of it, feeling the smoothness beneath my digit. I opened up the door inside of myself that let out the magical part of me and I had to fight to keep myself steady.

A necromancer had an affinity with the dead, it was just what we were, and death happened everywhere. If I concentrated hard enough I could trace every single death that had happened along this entire street. Considering the church at the end? That could be an awful lot of death. I wasn't looking just for death though. I was looking for a spirit that lingered. A ghost. I needed a human ghost.

The house was old. But the land it sat on top of was even older. People had died here, been buried near by. I saw glimpses of women in childbirth, of men brawling in the dark. I saw old men and women asleep in their beds. I saw children covered in sickness and animal slaughtered for meals. The land had changed over time, being a farm, being a cottage, being the house it was now. Death, old as can be, had been here, but not a lot of spirits lingered.

"Oh come on," I growled under my breath. I kept my eyes closed and focused on the tendrils of lingering spirits, trying to chase one back to its owner. I wasn't very good at this, it was like tugging on spider webs. Every time I got close to something the line would snap and wither away beneath my metaphysical fingers.

And then I found it, a line that snapped tight for me. I followed it. I didn't see anything, not really. I just got a slew of sensations. A male, tall and strong. I tugged and felt the undead come. It was weak, barely clinging to its current existence. I could fix that. My magic nourished the dead. I pushed my magic down that line, feeding the dead.

The dead, and their undead cousins, were a hungry bunch. The spirit at the end of my magic drank deeply. I let him, right up until my head started to spin.

"Come to me," I beckoned, not just with my words but with my will. The spirit paused. I said it again, firmer this time. It tried to pull away. That made me mad. I gave it magic and it wasn't going to help me? Oh no. Not today. Not this time. I had stuff to do.

I tugged again, and this time the spirit came.

For a moment, I thought I had messed up. After all, the spirit was coming from one of the creepy upstairs rooms. According to the visions I had just had, no one had died in these rooms. The door near the end of the hall was vibrating, buckling as if someone was throwing their weight against it. I couldn't hear anything though. I watched as the door vibrated, and then flew apart. I clapped my hands over my face to protect myself from pieces of wood and splinters of magic as they went flying everywhere.

When I looked up I went very still. It was a guy who stood before me, but it was in no way a ghost. This guy stood over six feet tall with the body of a brown Adonis. A good deal of it was on display too, since he was wearing boxer briefs and nothing else. There was a tightness around his eyes, sharp and angry. He glared down at me and I glared right back.

"Well," said a deep baritone voice, "this is the second time that you have saved me, Lorena Quinn." He didn't sound super happy about it.

"Zane...I thought you were dead."

His lips formed a tight line. On the average guy, it would have been an ugly look, but I was pretty sure that Zane couldn't look ugly. Angry, frustrated, and terrifying, yes. Ugly? Not so much. "I nearly was." He looked away. "You ruined it."

"I... I what?"

He snarled, and he was no longer handsome. His teeth lengthened inside of his mouth until fangs skimmed over his lips. His eyes went from dark brown to a startling red. A moment later a dark wind flooded over me, bringing with it the sensation of vampire magic. If I hadn't been a necromancer I would have stepped back.

"You ruined it!" he snarled. His voice reverberated across the hallway, echoing strangely. "You must have a gift for meddling. That's all you've ever done."

I rolled my eyes. "Yes, I'm the one meddling. You and that creepy cult are the one's trying to screw around with prophecy, but, hey. Let's put the blame on me."

He tried to surge forward, but the magic that I had used to summon him to me kept him in place. The tips of his hands were edged with pitch black claws. His skin was several shades darker than it had been.

"You would see the world remade!"

I shrugged. "And?"

"You would put my father and his whores into power."

I blinked. "I...huh?"

"Do not play the fool with me. I've seen you with Dmitri and Alan and Wei. My brothers have grown special to you."

I shrugged. "Yeah. So?"

"You will fall into the clutches of my father. You will set him on the throne of magic."

I wasn't following his line of logic here. "Okay, so that's totally not the plan."

"You have not met him! Women swoon to him, flock to him! They cannot resist the temptation of his smile and the sickly-sweet promises he whispers in their ears. They all go to him."

There was a whole wealth of bitterness in his words that had me taking a step back. Okay, part of that probably had something to do with the fact that I was pretty sure I was going to throw up. Just the thought of going to Vlad in any way was enough to make me feel nauseated. Ew. Just ew. Ew times a billion.

"Okay, two things. One, I've totally met Vlad."

His eyes went wide, and then they narrowed. "You are lost!"

"That's thing number two. Dude tried and failed."

"Liar!"

I shrugged. I really had no desire to sit her and explain why I was totally not interested in his creepy dad, but I found myself saying, "Have I ever lied to you?"

He seemed to think it over. For that matter, I did too. I wasn't a dishonest person by nature, but I wondered if I had ever lied to him about anything.

"What happened?" he demanded, as if he wanted more proof.

"Dude..."

"What happened!" he snapped at me. I jumped.

"Don't you make commands of me," I snapped right back. My fists clenched at my sides. "You aren't my father, you aren't my boyfriend. Hell! You're the creep who lied to me to get me to go out on a date with him in case you've forgotten."

"I had good reasons."

"Yeah, I'm sure. And I'm also sure those reasons all revolved around the idea that you knew a better way of dealing with this stupid prophecy, right?" When he didn't immediately answer I took a step towards him, taking back the ground that I had given up. "Right?"

"Yes."

I threw up my hands. "Yeah, that's what I thought. You know what? I'm so tired of this crap. I'm so tired of everyone, literally everyone thinking that they know what's best for me. Literally from the moment I was born everyone has been making the decisions for me and I am done."

"Your father-" he started.

"My father, my mother, my sister. The Order. You. Heck, you wanna get bitchy about your vampire daddy trying to ensnare me, but dude, you are no better."

"What are you saying?"

I don't know why I told him. I don't know why it all came spilling out, but it did. I told him everything that had happened from the moment I had woken up in bed, with him and Wei missing to the moment that I had walked into the house. Somewhere during the tirade, I had plopped down on the ground, mist swirling all around me.

I don't know who was more surprised when he sat down next to me, him or myself, but I was absolutely floored when his arms came around me.

"I am sorry."

I tensed. The last time he had been nice to me it was all a lie. "For what?"

"For thinking you were weak."

He hadn't been the only one, but I couldn't bring myself to say that out loud. I was definitely tired of people thinking that they knew what I should do rather than just letting me make my own decisions.

"I can't trust you."

He gave my shoulders a squeeze. I think he was trying to be comforting. It would have been more comforting if he was wearing pants. "I can help you."

"How?" I knew there was only one thing that he could say that would let me let him help me.

"I know where Wei is."

Yeah. That was the thing.

CHAPTER EIGHT

"Where is he?" I demanded. I stood up fast enough to jerk out of Zane's embrace, which is pretty impressive when one of us had supernatural strength and the other didn't. "Who has him?"

Okay, I had some guesses to those questions, but they were just guesses. I didn't actually know. For all I knew Wei had been taken by aliens to a tropical planet on the other side of the Andromeda galaxy. Zane's lips turned into a grim line.

"If I tell you will you release me from your necromancer's hold?"

I had absolutely no idea what a necromancer's hold was, much less that I had him in one. But now that I was thinking about it I could feel the magic that bound him to me like an invisible leash. I felt a little guilty about it, but then I remembered that he had lied to me and played with my feelings. I felt a little less bad. "Not until I know the information you have pans out."

"What does that mean?" I didn't know his lips could get into a thinner line, but they did.

"Until I have proof that you aren't lying. I don't know if you know this but pretty much our entire relationship has been based on lies and that's just not okay with me." I threw my hands up into the air. "Jeez, were you even in trouble when I rescued you the first time?"

He turned his head to the side, his already thin mouth forming into a razor-sharp frown. "Yes."

I felt a tinge of shock. "So, what? My sister tricked you into being a ritual sacrifice and then?" I needed to understand. If someone I had been sweet on wanted to steal all of my blood for some screwed up ritual I'd have to say bye. That was just one of my deal breakers. No smoking, no drugs, no ritual sacrifice. I'm weird that way.

"I love her," he said, and I wasn't sure if he was talking to himself or me.

"Dude..." I shook my head. I wanted to tell him that he deserved better. Maybe he did. I liked to think that I knew Zane, but I wasn't entirely sure that was true. "Where is he?"

"Your mother has him. And she is keeping him at the temple."

I had not been right about the who or the where. "Wait. What? My mom? He's not at the compound?"

"You know the location of the compound; do you honestly believe that your mother would keep him there?" He gave me a mocking look.

He had a point, but he didn't have to say it like that. "Okay. Fine. So why mother dearest? I would have put my money on Connie."

"You killed her lover."

Oh. Right. That. I had played a pretty major role in the death of the leader of the Order, who had also been my mom's boy toy, but to be fair, he had started it.

"She's going to kill Wei?" I asked. "Wait, she's had him for months, why wouldn't she kill him already?"

"Markus lingered for weeks in his coma, and your mother knows that he was in pain the entire time." His words were careful, and for just a moment his eyes stopped being red and went back to their normal tiger's eye brown.

Markus, who I had nicknamed Creepy Dude about two point five seconds after I had met him, was the recently deceased lover of my mother, and the father to my half-sister Connie. He had also been the leader of the cult known as the Order of the Loyal Hermit, who liked to think that I was pretty much the anti-Christ to their way of thinking. He'd had me locked in a room after my mom had used her magic to kidnap me from one of the few nights out that I had. When I had broken out there had been a fight, he was injured. I hadn't known how bad the injury was, but it had been enough to put him into a coma.

"Yeah, well, he took that pain out on me." I couldn't muster up any pity for Markus the Creepy Dude. He had tried to trap me in my own dreams before he died.

He shrugged. "It doesn't matter, she still blames you, and she will take all of her misery out on him."

"How does Connie factor into this?"

"He was her father," he said. "They were never close, but now she does not have the chance to try to be."

They had seemed close enough to me, but I guess that I didn't know much. "So what? They have Wei in some temple? Jeez, he's been there for a month?"

Zane couldn't quite meet my eyes. "Your mother is in pain, and your sister is vengeful." He paused before he said, "a vampire can take a great deal of pain before they die."

His words hit me like a hammer. Wei. My beautiful, stubborn Wei. It had been a month since he disappeared. A month. My mother's magics tended towards mental manipulation, my sister had an affinity with beasts and, if the ritual she'd put Zane through had anything to show me, blood. What had they done to him? A hundred terrible images flickered through my mind. I felt a wave of sickness roll through me. I swallowed it. There would be time for getting sick later. I had stuff to do.

"Where is the temple?"

"You cannot go there."

"Why the heck not?"

He gave me a look that told me just what he thought of how little I knew. It bothered me. The Zane I knew had been a nice person, not the kind to sling dark looks at everyone. Then again, the Zane I had known had been a lie.

"The Temple of the Order of the Loyal Hermit is a fortress."

I remembered the compound, which seemed more like a school for the Order, it was a big square building behind an impressive fence that looked more like some military fort than anything comfortable. "Sounds about right."

"It's a fortress," he repeated. "You'd need a whole army to get in. Even then..."

I shrugged. *I was just going to have to find an army, wasn't I?* I added that to my mental to-do list and rolled my shoulders in preparation. "You tell me where it is. Leave the rest to me."

He chewed on his lower lip and then hung his head. "You'll hurt her."

"Huh?"

His head snapped up, and flicks of crimson red chased the natural golden-brown hue of his eyes. "If you go to the Temple, if you go for Wei, you are going to hurt Connie."

Well, that was probably true. I'd like to pretend it wasn't going to happen that way, but it would be a lie. She hated me, I wasn't all that fond of her. There was a pretty high chance that me assaulting the Order's base of operations was going to end in a throw down and Connie and I were probably going to be involved. Epic boss battles and all that. "I don't want to."

It was true enough. I didn't want to hurt Connie. I didn't want to hurt my mom. I didn't have a whole lot of family. Just my dad. The truth was, before all of this started, I used to imagine having a big family.

One that could take up a whole dining table, not just two chairs of it. I used to imagine a loving mother who cared about me, and a sibling, usually a sister, I could be best friends with. I didn't get that. I got creepy mom and angry sister and both of them wanted me to not fulfill my destiny. It was a sticking point.

"You might not, but it will happen." He sounded so sure.

"What do you want me to do? Let her kill Wei? Let her kill me?" I gave a laugh empty of any real humor. "Not gonna happen."

"Let me go with you."

I blinked in shock. "Wait, what? You want to come with me?" I shook my head. "Nope. No, no, no. I've played enough video games to know how this works out. I show the enemy a little trust, one of them comes with me to show me a secret way into the Arch Villain's super-secret base and I end up going right to the boss battle where the helper shows their true face and I end up getting my butt whooped. Nope. Noooo." I shook my head again, hard enough to make my ash brown hair bounce. "Hard pass."

"You have to!" he snapped. His eyes were still glittering and red. Jeez, how had I ever gone out with him? He was scary. Not quite Dmitri in a rage scary, but scary enough. Sure, we got along and cuddling had been nice, but jeez, I dodged a bullet on this one.

I held up a single finger, showing him just how intimidated I was. "Here's the thing. I totally don't. I don't have to do anything. I don't have to take you anywhere. I can leave you in this creepy place where the mist smells like a dog who rolled around in swamp water." My voice didn't even shake when I said it. Bad ass points for me.

"I know the layout of the temple. I know the strengths and weaknesses of everyone who dwells within. You cannot take the temple without my help."

"Yeah, see, here's another thing. The whole reason I am here is to get help. Jenny is in one of these rooms, and you are going to help me get to her."

He gave me another long look. His eyes glittered like rubies and some emotion passed through them that had me wanting to take a step back. "Not if you don't promise to take me with you."

"Why?" I wanted to know. "Why does it matter so much to you if you go? So what if I hurt Connie. I hate to point this out, but the girl totally hurt you. Like...a lot." I remembered how he had looked stretched out on the strange blood sucking apparatus all those weeks ago. He had been gray with blood loss and skinny. *Well*, I thought looking down at his bare legs, *he was still skinny*. But now he was healthy skinny rather than sick skinny and those were two really different things.

"I love her," he snarled. He shuddered when he said it, like he hated himself for saying it.

"You are insane." I rolled my eyes. "She tried to kill you. Heck...is she the person who put you in this creepy place?" I waved my hands about in the general direction of the broken door.

He frowned at me. "Yes." His shoulder sagged forward.

"Then you are extra insane. Dude, when a girl tries to sacrifice you for her beliefs she isn't interested in keeping you. Move on. This isn't healthy."

"It is not that easy."

"Why not?"

"I am a vampire." He said it like that had more meaning than I understood.

"What does that have to do with anything?" Inquiring minds needed to know, what with me being in love with a vampire and all.

"Do you believe that a vampire is merely a human turned blood drinker?" he asked. His eyes went bright as rubies. "Do you think there is no difference between mortals and immortals but the span of our lives? We are other. We do not seek out the companionship of humans. They are too short lived to bond with, to connect ourselves to.. They can offer us nothing than a glimpse of what we once were. They are, at their very best, a pleasant bit of food, and at worst a painful mirror to show us all that we have lost."

His eyes were growing bright enough to cast ruby tinted shadows across the walls. The mist seemed to glow red around us. "But every now and then, Lorena, every now and then there comes a human whom makes us remember what it is like to care. Their presence makes our dead hearts ache with the desire to beat for them. It is a rare thing, once a millennium if you are very very lucky. The presence of this person is the one and only thing we crave more than blood. It is what used to drive Vlad to create more wives and children for himself, and had I the ability I would make your sister mine for all of eternity. It goes beyond the fleeting idea of human love which can last for the shortness of your lifetime, but the bond that only an immortal can truly understand."

His words didn't just catch me by surprise. They threw me for a loop. I stood there, absolutely dumbfounded. Was that what Wei felt when he looked at me? There was a part of me that didn't like that, not a little, not even at all. I didn't feel that way about Wei. I loved him. I loved those secret smiles he had and the way he looked when he practiced his martial arts, but he didn't make me feel alive any more than a binge session of my favorite television show did. Oh boy. "Oh." I swallowed twice. "And. you are sure you feel this for my sister?"

"Yes."

"But does she feel it about you?" I asked, because I was pretty sure I knew the answer to that one.

"It doesn't matter if she does or does not," he said, "love does not have to be returned to matter."

He gave me a look that told me he thought I was an idiot. I held my hands up in surrender and rolled my eyes. "Whatever, dude."

"Now, will you let me join you?" His nose flared as if he was taking in deep and ragged breaths, but I knew better. He was a vampire and they didn't need to breathe.

I wasn't sure it was a good idea, but I nodded. "Help me get through these doors, and you can come with us. I still think you are a fool, but," I shrugged. "Love makes people foolish or something like that." I motioned to the door behind him. "I need to get through these doors."

He turned from me, and I could see the tense line of his shoulders bunch and curl as he inspected the same symbols on the doors that I had. "These are magical runes."

"No, duh. I knew that much. I just don't know how to get through them. I was trying to find a ghost to help me, I got you instead."

"A ghost?" he asked, still keeping his eye on the door.

"Yeah, you know. Preferably named Casper or something equally friendly. Just something to help me see what's on the other side of that door, maybe knew more about magical runes than I did."

He snorted. "What use is a witch who doesn't know runes?"

"Dude, back off," I snapped. "I have been at this all of two months and in that time, I've been kidnapped, dream-napped, and attacked by the father of all vampires. I deserve a gold star for putting up with everything that I have and not freaking out on, you know, everyone."

He was quiet for a moment. "There are witches past this door."

I had figured that much out, but I kept that to myself. "Okay, but how do we get past the door without me getting zapped like a fly?"

"Magic."

I wanted to tear my hair out.

"No sh-"

"Raw magic," he cut me off. "You will need to overpower the runes, spill raw magic into them until they break. Think of it like a balloon filling with water. It may expand, but it will only hold so much."

There was a certain amount of logic there, but even so I was still unsure. "They'll explode."

"Probably, but it will be a controlled explosion."

Well, it was better than my idea, which was throw stuff at the door until the magic broke. "Okay, stand back."

He shifted down the side of the wall, and waited.

Magic is weird. I don't say that to sound all crazy or mystical or whatever. I say it because it's true. There are a few basic rules I have learned in the inanely short time I've been practicing, most of which can boil down to don't be a jerk with magic, but I was pretty sure that pouring magic into magic runes in order to make them explode was breaking some rule somewhere. But what could I do? Short answer? Nothing. Long answer? Just do it.

I took a deep breath and raised my hand so that it hovered just over the inscriptions. My fingers were still tingling from the first shock I had. I was really hoping that I wasn't about to experience the full body version. I closed my eyes and opened up that door that separated me from where my magic lived. The door hadn't really been closed, I still had a tendril of it snaked around Zane, but it wasn't really open either. It was more like a faucet that had been barely left on, and now I had to turn everything up to full power.

I summed up my magic and the tingle in my arm went away. Zane hissed behind me, but I ignored it. I focused on the shape of the runes and symbols beneath my hand, and pushed the magic into them.

It hurt. Not as much as getting blasted across the room, but the magic that had been used on the door did not like being messed with and it made me very aware of that. It felt like needles poking back at me, like some sort of invisible porcupine. Not fun. But I persisted. I needed to know what was behind that door and I really hoped that it would help.

Magic pulsed around me like a wave, it crashed around me, but not against me. I kept shoving my essence against the magic, filling up the symbols into they shivered beneath my palm. Air pressure filled the hallway. My ears popped. And then the explosion happened. Or rather, implosion. Nothing went out, everything seemed to warp towards the circle of the door and then disappear completely. The moment it did I sagged to my knees.

"Well," I said, breathing hard, "that went better than I expected."

I tilted my head, and peered into the room beyond.

CHAPTER NINE

When you break past a magical circle to get into a room that is spilling acrid mist out into a too long hallway that shouldn't exist, you pretty much prepare yourself to see anything. Okay, I thought, almost anything.

It was not a room that existed beyond the door, but a swamp. Elegant trees with roots invested in constantly wet soil were heavy with Spanish moss. The moss was long enough to stroke the surface of the nearly green water. The scent of wet dog and moldy things was strong here. A single beam of moonlight illuminated what looked to be a pier. A small motorless boat was attached to it by the length of moldy rope.

"Okay," I said. "That's different."

I felt Zane move up behind me. My magic reverberated with his nearness. "It's a swamp witch's ream," he said, his voice a hushed rumble.

I bet it was, not that I really knew what a swamp witch was. "Why would there be a magical door to a swamp witch's dream world inside the house of Marquessa Green? That's…ridiculous. Right?" Not that anything in my life hadn't been ridiculous recently.

"You misunderstand, I mean it is literally a witch's dream." He lifted his nose and sniffed at the air. "I can smell it."

"Dude, how can you smell anything but wet dog?" I demanded.

I looked over my shoulder and he shrugged. For a moment, his dark eyes stared into my hazel ones and I felt the urge to ask him about my sister. What was it that he saw in her? Why was he doing this for someone who had hurt him so much?

"We won't know unless we go inside," he said, interrupting my train of thought.

He was right, but the fact that he was the one who said it had me hesitating. I still didn't trust him. I took one step over the threshold and felt the soggy ground squish beneath my boot.

"Hey, so before you follow me into the world of swamp dream magic-" God, that sounded absurd even to me- "maybe you ought to find some pants."

Zane looked down at himself, as if only just now realizing that he wasn't fully clothed. The Zane I knew liked to be clothed. In fact, on our one and only date he had been dressed from Adam's apple to toe. It had all been very attractive, but if I was being honest, Zane could probably have been wearing a paper bag and be hot.

"I might have something in the room I was in." His hands were clasped in front of him to hide his dignity.

I waited. He didn't move. I waited some more.

"Well are you going to go get it?" I asked.

He gave me a sneer. "I cannot."

"Why?"

He looked down at the invisible lines that tethered us together, the magic neither of us could see but we could both feel.

"You hold the reins." he snarled.

I couldn't be mad at him for being pissy about it. Heck, I wouldn't have liked someone to have the magical whammy on me either, but I didn't trust him enough to let him go.

"Right," I took a deep breath and concentrated on the line. "Go get your clothes from the room you were being held in."

He turned and walked away. The line would let him do just what I asked and no more. I wish I could say I didn't watch him go, but the view was too good not to give an appreciative look. When he returned with clothes in his hand, but not dressed I realized I should have worded my command better.

He must have seen my thoughts on my face. "This would be a great deal easier if you relinquished the hold."

"I don't trust you," I said.

"You will need your magic for other things," he reminded me. "And I will be accompanying you anyway."

I shook my head. "Yeah, that whole thing sounds good and logical right up until you realize the easiest way to keep your creepy girlfriend from getting hurt is to push me off a cliff or something. Just get dressed and let's go. I'm a little freaked out that I can't smell wet dog anymore." I was pretty sure that my nose had just grown accustomed to the smell, but that didn't make me feel any better.

I turned around to give Zane a bit of privacy as he pulled his clothes on. The brief pause had my brain going a million miles an hour. Did Wei feel for me the way Zane felt for Connie? Was he being punished for feeling what he did? Was everything that was going on my fault? Ugh. I didn't like these thoughts. I wanted them to go away. I wanted things to be simple and easy. I wanted to sit on a couch with my vampire boyfriend and play video games and remake the world in magic.

A hand landed on my shoulder and I jumped. When I whirled around, absolutely sure that Zane was about to push me into the swamp or something equally villainous I was struck by the sadness in his eyes.

"You are worried for him." He didn't ask it, he said it. He was dressed now, and I was sure the clothes were his, a dark gray button-down shirt and a pair of deep brown slacks. While the other vampires liked to dress in stereotypes, Zane dressed like casual

Friday at the CEO's lounge. It was always khakis or other slacks, and button-down shirts or expensive turtlenecks. Of all the vampires, his clothes seemed to be the most modern. I wondered why that was, considering I had been told he was the eldest of the brothers.

I shrugged. "What was your first clue?"

He reached a hand out and dabbed the wetness of my cheek. Great. I had gotten so used to crying that I didn't even realize when I did it now. Fan-friggen-tastic. He gave me a gentle look and I resisted the urge to cry some more. What was it about people being nice when I felt like crap that made me want to cry? Not cool.

I swiped angrily at my cheeks and took a step away from him. "Come on."

Maahes sprang in front of me, his tail curling as he started to walk along the edge of the swamp water. His ghostly feet didn't make a single dip in the ground as he moved. I started to follow.

"Are we going to follow the cat?" he asked dubiously.

I shrugged. "That cat has a name, and yes. So far Maahes hasn't led me wrong." We lapsed into silence as the swamp stretched out in front of us. When I couldn't take the sound of my feel on soggy ground anymore I asked, "how can this be a dream? I've been involved in dream magic before and you have to be asleep for it."

"You do when it's somniamancy. But it is not the only magic that can produce a dream world."

Great. More stuff about magic that everyone else seemed to know but me. "What else does it?"

He didn't answer at first. I looked over my shoulder at him, but he wasn't giving me that insufferable look that I was expecting. Instead he was looking over my shoulder, past me to something that lay beyond. I had a sudden urge to stay completely still. It was as if my body was telling me that if I didn't look at whatever had Zane's eyes glittering, I wouldn't see what had the vampire preparing himself for battle.

"Don't...move," he whispered.

I didn't. I didn't even want to breathe. Maahes had hunkered down by my legs, his ears pinned back and the tip of his tail flicking like an anxious bird. It matched the beating of my heart. A fierce rumble reverberated out of his throat, sounding even more eerie because of the mist.

"What's going on?" I asked, so quietly that it would take a vampire's acute senses to hear me.

"Swamp hag." He breathed the word, barely giving it any sound. If I had not been looking right at his mouth, watching the movement of his lips, I would not have been able to figure out what he was saying at all.

I flipped through the files of my memory until I came across the one about Hags. I had read about them in my grandmother's book. Okay, okay. I had skimmed about them. I was not the best student in the world. There is a chance I'm lazy. I'm working on it...you know...after I recreate the world with magic.

Hags were corrupted witches. Witches who, through some action usually involving blood sacrifices or forbidden magics, had bound themselves to other entities or creatures who gave them more power. It sounded like a great deal until you realize that the hag now corrupted the very land she walked on because she had done something terrible, something the very world couldn't abide.

I probably should have paid better attention, because I was pretty sure that a hag was a witch's greatest enemy or something. Yeah, I definitely should have researched that more.

"What do I do?"

"Have you ever dueled a hag?" he asked.

"What? You mean like pistols at dawn? Ten paces? All that crap?" I hissed between my teeth.

He gave me a look that told me that I had the complete wrong idea. Yeah, I wasn't surprised. I was one hundred percent sure that I had the wrong idea.

"Get behind me."

"What?" I demanded.

"Get. Behind. Me." He punctuated every word, as if I couldn't understand them as a sentence, but might as individual sounds. I was not amused.

"Dude-"

"Lorena, now."

I was just about to tell him that I was the necromancer here and he couldn't order me to do anything when Maahes gave an almighty hiss. I whirled around and saw her, at least I was assuming it was a her, she barely looked human. She had two arms and two legs and one head, but that was about where the similarity stopped. Her back was curled over so much that her body looked more like a question mark with a lump growing out of the top. Her arms were too thin, and had the gnarled look of branches. They swayed like willow limbs as she walked. Her dress, barely more than a belted sack, hung on a lumpy body, and all of it was held up on two legs that would have looked more at home on a chicken.

She peered at us through a curtain of moldy hair. Her lips, thin and green, formed into a knife sharp smile. Fear froze my blood in my veins before she threw her head back and let out a wild shriek of laughter. I wasn't frozen anymore.

My legs were moving before I even thought. The ground was too wet and soggy beneath my frantic steps. I went knees first into the swamp ground and my pants became soaked in moss covered earth. It was not as pretty as it sounded. Truth? It hurt. Shocks of pain radiated up into my hip and then my back. I crawled like a crab behind Zane as another laughing shriek surged up behind me.

Zane had changed. I had seen vampires shift before. Dmitri and Yasmina had become more beast that human when they prepared for battle. Alan and his sister had been quick as lashes when given the opportunity. I had even seen Zane fight before, and I had heard from all of his brothers that he was the most powerful of them, as first born he was the closest to Vlad in strength. Even with all that I still didn't expect the guy I saw before me.

His muscles stood out beneath skin the color of a shadow. Not brown, but black. A rich dark black that you got on a moonless night. His eyes were like red suns glimmering out of his angular face. His teeth were elongated and sharp, making twin pearl points over his full lips. He was beautiful and terrifying.

A few weeks ago, he had saved me. Dmitri had gone a little bonkers, as the more primal vampires tend to, and I had been pretty sure I was done for. Then Zane had come out of nowhere and rescued me. He had called himself the Shadow, and now I could see why.

"Little witch, little witch, come out to play." The hag's voice was like wet bark, grating against one another. She spoke with the sing-song tone of a nursery rhyme as she peered at me around the dark line of Zane's body. "Come out and play."

"Nope." I shook my head. "Nooo. Hard pass. Not gonna happen. I'm totally grounded."

She frowned at me. "You decline?"

She said decline like it should be capitalized. I blinked. "Yes?"

Her already ugly face twisted until it would have done Picasso proud. A shrill scream reverberated through the swamp. The mist swirled around us forming a hurricane of smoky air. The scent of old dog surged up around me. My head went light. It thickened until I could barely see. All I saw was a swirl around me before the mist engulfed me completely. This was not where I wanted to be. All I could see was the shadow of Zane's body in front of me. Maahes was completely invisible.

My eyes fluttered closed and for just a moment I forgot what I was doing here. Fear leeched out of me. My body felt like rubber. I wanted to lay down. God, I was tired. I was so tired. And why wouldn't I be? Everything was wrong and nothing I did ever seemed to help. I didn't belong here. I belonged back at the burger joint, listening to people yell at me for not having the ice cream machine up at eleven thirty at night. I was just a gamer. I couldn't even make it in college. I took a deep breath and slithered to the ground. I didn't care that the wet, soggy ground was ruining my jeans. I didn't deserve to have them.

I heard the slap of flesh against flesh. I looked up and saw a dark shadow grabbing a green one. A clawed fist slammed down, and the hunched figure went to her knees. But then her hands shot out and Zane went flying. His dark body slammed against a tree.

"The dead are foolish to walk in my domain."

Hey. That wasn't cool. Zane was alright. Yeah, he was a lying vampire but he was my lying vampire and if anyone was going to send him halfway across a swamp clearing it was going to be me. Another wave of mist washed over me and I was overwhelmed with the same self-loathing ennui I had been a moment ago. I shook my head. Crap. It was the mist. It was messing with my head.

Zane lunged at the hag again and managed another strike, but this time it barely seemed to hurt her. When the moonlight hanging between the Spanish moss caught her face I could see that her skin had changed. It was more like bark than flesh. When Zane's usually lethal claws hit her skin, he scraped off wood. She laughed, a high shrill sound and returned the strike. Zane didn't move, but her hand, tipped with twig like claws, hit nothing but smoke.

It was like watching two titans fight. One made of wood and stone, the other made of smoke and mist. Each hit did so little damage it was as if nothing was happening at all. It should have made me feel better, it didn't. Zane was a vampire, and that gave him more stamina than most, but he'd been locked up in a room for who knew how long and his weakness showed. No, I thought. It didn't show. The shadow of his movements masked everything, but I could feel it in the connection that we shared. He was weakening and it was happening quick.

I could help. I don't know why it took me so long to remember, I blamed my brain being scared witless, but the dead were my domain. My magic sought them like water to the river, or something as equally poetic. I could summon them. I could command them. But those weren't the first tricks I had learned. The first one had been my ability to invigorate them. I could pump a vampire so full of energy that it was like he'd been eating five course meals and preparing for a triathlon.

I opened that connection between Zane and I. My magic traveled down that line until I was so aware of him that I wasn't sure where he started and I began. I could feel his exhaustion. It wasn't like human exhaustion. Vampires didn't breathe or sleep. It was more like a pile of bricks had been laid on his shoulders and he was still trying to move. He shook beneath the weight of it.

I summoned up that energy that made me a necromancer, the magic that felt like ozone and summer nights on my skin. I pushed it down that connection, spilled it into him like he was a cup. He jerked when it hit him, stumbled down on one knee. For a moment, I thought that he was upset. His shoulders became a set, rigid line and his shadowy head bowed. Then I felt his gratitude. The hag slammed her hand down, aiming for a strike to the back of his neck. In a faster move than I could follow he snapped his hand around her wrist and yanked. I heard the snap of a branch and dimly realized that was her arm breaking. She trilled her pain and lashed out with her free hand, catching him across the cheek. He didn't shift to shadow and I felt my own head jerk with the pain that I felt.

Anger suffused us. How dare she strike us. How dare she not know when she had lost. Only a fool did not realize when the fight was over. It was far better to bow to a greater opponent than to hurtle yourself against insurmountable odds.

It was so strange to be in a vampire's mind, or maybe it was just Zane's. I had touched the minds of vampires before, it was how I knew that Wei loved me. My own brain was liable to run around with thoughts until everything was a great big tangled web. His mind was so organized. I could follow each thought to the inevitable conclusion. She had lost, he had won, and it was idiotic that she hadn't realized it yet. I wondered what it was like to live with that kind of confidence.

He slammed an open palm into her bark like face. There was another crack of branches. It wasn't blood that spurted out of her nose, but something thicker, more like sap. Her head snapped back and she would have crumpled to the ground were it not for the way he still held her broken arm.

"Stop!" she cried. "Stop! I relent. You win." She held her hands up in submission.

He still held her. We wanted to break her neck. We didn't trust her. I shook my head. Now that things weren't so hectic I could separate his thoughts from my own. I could feel that he didn't believe her, that he thought it was a trap or some kind of trick. He didn't say it out loud. Instead he held her and turned his glimmering eyes on me. What did I want to do, he seemed to ask.

"Who are you?" I asked.

She looked at me. The sap had filled the cracks of her face. "They call me Dora, at least they did years ago. Now I am traitor, and hag."

I didn't need to ask who "they" was. I assumed that it was other witches. "Because you made a compact?" I asked, curiosity overriding my other worries. I might be a lazy student, but that didn't mean I didn't want to understand.

She laughed. "The Green Man needed a herald, and I was more than willing to give myself to his clutches."

A Green Man, now that was something I had read about. Every forest, or bastion of wild greenery, had a Green Man who protected it. He was some kind of fae and it was his place to protect where the wilds were still free of man. My grandmother's journal had said that they were extinct, or at least on the way to being extinct.

"There are no Green Men," Zane said. "They left when the Queen of Fae called her people home."

Okay, more information. What the heck. What I knew about the Fae could fit on one side of an index card. I knew that they had a Queen, and that she ruled them for a few thousand years or something like that. That was pretty much all I knew.

Her wooden lips curled into a smile. "Not mine. Not mine. He did not wish to leave me, nor the swamp we had tended together. But we couldn't survive, could we? Not alone, not apart. We needed each other. And so we bound ourselves together. Him to me and back again." She shuddered as if she was remembering a particularly good kiss. "We shared our essence."

I felt a desire to blush and I wasn't entirely sure I understood why.

"You committed a blasphemy of magic," Zane spat.

She shrugged her good shoulder. "Is there something you would not do for love, vampire?"

I felt an image of my sister's face flash into Zane's mind. She looked soft in his memories, one arm throw over her head as she slept. Her freckles looked like stars to him. Her lips were pale rose petals. I wasn't surprised to see her. What I was surprised to see was a brief glimpse of myself, curled up with him on the couch. He locked the thoughts down and away from me and I blinked at the sudden lack of contact.

What the heck had that been about? I shook my head, unwilling to think about it. I had enough on my plate without wondering if Zane was beginning to have conflicting feelings.

"I wouldn't corrupt myself for it." I shook my head. "Not for anything."

She laughed. "How do you think you will bare a vampire's child? They are dead, you know. They cannot bring life without life being brought to them."

Honestly? I hadn't thought of that. I had just kind of assumed that there was some spell or something that would let that whole thing happen. Was she right? Was I going to have to bind myself to a vampire to make this whole prophecy thing happen? Oh crap. I shook my head. No. She couldn't be right, she couldn't possibly be right.

She smiled that knife-like smile and gave a cackle that sounded like branches caught in a hurricane wind. Her nose had stopped bleeding but the lines of her lower face were still filled with that strange ichor.

"Oh, you foolish little witch. Did your teacher not tell you?" The look on my face must have given me away. "You don't have a teacher, do you?"

"I did." I snapped. "I had two of them. You took them. They are here somewhere. Where are they? Where are we?" All the questions that had been building up came out of my mouth in a tumble. I wasn't going to be distracted by her tidbits of knowledge.

She tsked and shook her head sadly. "If your teachers had been worthy of your loyalty, they would have told you all about pocket dimensions and witches' travel."

Pocket dimensions sounded like something I should be hunting for through a temporarily popular phone app.

"I don't understand."

She tugged on her broken arm and Zane gave me another look. I gave him the barest of nods and he dropped her to the ground. She crumpled into a pile of spindly limbs, but righted herself quickly enough.

"It used to be when a witch got strong enough she could use her magic to create a place just for her. It wasn't very large, but it was necessary. After all, once upon a time, people would come to us for all manner of things -- charms, rituals, knowledge; both humans and otherwise. We were the crux between the world of magic and the mundane. We needed a place to be ours, to get away from it all.

What it was depended on the witch. Yours might be a cemetery under a full moon, or a little house in the middle of nowhere where it was perpetually autumn. It would be entirely up to you. You could take all the time you needed.

We could bring whomever we wanted there, make what we needed. All the time in all the world was ours to be had in these places. But when magic started to fail, so too did our dimensions." She spat the word, and a hunk of that drying ichor to the ground. "But when I bound myself to my Green Man..." she spread her fingers wide and swept them in a semi-circle.

"If this is yours, how are we here?"

She laughed. "Well, that's Marquessa's fault, isn't it? She tried to bring us all together."

My heart did a little leap. "Marquessa did this?"

"No, but she found the witch who could. One who could summon us all at once. It didn't go well." She rubbed her wounded arm.

"What do you mean?" I demanded, feeling more confused than ever.

"Witches are solitary creatures by nature, little witch. We enjoy our solitude and we do not much enjoy it being interrupted. Ornery women were disrupted." She shrugged and waved a hand towards the broken door that I could still see behind me. "And all of this ensued."

"I still don't understand. Are you saying that Marquessa found a witch that could summon you all, that this witch did, and all of those doors are pockets to dimensions?"

Dora nodded, her willow-like hair moving around her face. "Is that not what I said?"

I wanted to tell her no, that most of this I was piecing together through bits and pieces of what she had said and my own knowledge, but I didn't. "And that some of them took offense to being uprooted and a bitch fest went down and that ended....how?"

She sighed. "We fought, and magics combined, as they are inclined to do, and some are stuck."

"Stuck?"

"Mmm." She plucked at her scrap of a dress. "Stuck."

I blew out a breath. "Great. Something else to add to my to-do list."

This was like one of those open world video games were the quests just kept piling up and I wasn't sure how I was going to get everything done before I got to the main quest. I jerked my hand through my hair and growled. "Okay. So, do you know where Marquessa and Jenny Green are?"

She shrugged her shoulders. "Not here."

That had me pausing. "Who is here?"

She gave me a wicked smile, but didn't answer me. I didn't even need to give Zane a look for him to swipe Dora up. She gave a protesting squeak. "Only the Frenchman!" She said Frenchman like it was a title. Then her lips shifted so the creepy smile became an even creepier grin. "He could help you."

I snorted. "uh-huh."

"He has the same affinity for the dead that you carry. He could teach you many things."

I have to admit it. I paused. I knew so little about my own magic, and the lore about necromancy was very, very low. Most of the books I had thumbed through had little more than a paragraph about what I could do and it usually boiled down to "can raise the dead". Everything that I was doing came from instinct, not knowledge, and instinct was only going to get me so far.

"What do you want?" I asked, knowing that it wouldn't come without some kind of strings.

"Let me go," she shrugged. "That's all I ask. I have never hurt anyone. I wish only to be returned to my Green Man and my home."

"She should die," Zane said. "She will only be more difficult in the future."

She gave Zane a look. "I have never been difficult to anyone who did not tread on my own lands. And, given the right education, I could never stand up to a necromancer of prophecy. Have you any clue how powerful you could be, witchling?"

Temptation beat around me like a storm. I was really tired of not knowing what my magic could do, and I was really tired of being the weakest witch.

"Show me the necromancer first."

"Lorena!" Zane snapped. "She is a hag! She is lying." His brilliantly gold eyes were filled with disbelief.

"I never lie," she hissed. "Not once has a lie passed my lips. The truth is terrifying enough."

He shook her and her wounded arm snapped back and forth like a branch caught in a breeze. She heaved out a whimper of pain.

"Zane, stop!" I cried out. "This is my decision to make."

He stopped as if I had hit pause. The look he gave me was filled with anger. "I forgot," he snarled, and I didn't need the tether between us to feel the anger radiating off of him. "I am your thrall." I could tell by the way he said it that "thrall" was not the first word he had wanted to say. A sick feeling slithered through my belly. It was true enough, my magic kept him tethered to me, took away his choices. I felt bad for it, but I was also too afraid of what he would do without it there. He was my undead slave, and it was wrong.

He dropped her to the ground with more force than was necessary. She managed to look both amused and offended.

"Come along," she said, beckoning with a hand that looked a little less like a branch and a little more like flesh. "I will show you where he slumbers."

I followed. I knew Zane didn't want to go, but after a moment he fell into step beside me. Dora was humming as she walked over soggy ground and raised roots. I stumbled in her wake. On a particularly bad one, Zane caught me.

"Thanks," I said as he helped me over the roots. He didn't answer so I continued. "I'm sorry for the...enthrallment."

He snorted. "Are you?"

"I am," I answered. "I wish it didn't need to be there. I wish I weren't afraid of you. I wish we were friends."

"You fear me?" he asked, sounding annoyed. "You could command me with a wave of your hand and you claim to be afraid of me."

I stepped over a fallen branch that seemed to squirm out of my path. "You are stronger than me, faster than me. You've got that mist thing going for you. Not to mention that whole immortal thing. And at the end of the day you are in love with my sister...who wants me dead. I think I'd be stupid not to be afraid of you."

He was quiet again, but there wasn't the same weight. "She is not so terrible as you believe."

I couldn't help but roll my eyes. "Are you serious? I mean, really? The girl spent the first few weeks I knew her pretending to be my friend. And when my mom decided to use her mental magics to kidnap me Connie helped set it up. I'm not an idiot. There is only one way my mom could have found us at the club. My sister betrayed us. And then there was the fact that she was willing to drain you of your life to change the prophecy? I mean, I don't know how you are the one who is still pining after her."

"She's dedicated," he insisted. "She believes in her cause. I cannot hold that against her."

I sighed and shook my head. "I dunno. Seems to me if the person I love is willing to drain me of everything that keeps me alive for their cause..."

"I know she does not love me as I love her," he interrupted. I stumbled again and this time his hands weren't half so gentle when he righted me. Instead he whirled me around and I found myself looking into his eyes. I expected them to be red, but they were his normal gold flecked with copper and yellow. So far as I could tell all vampires had beautiful eyes. Maybe it was a prerequisite. His hands gripped my upper arms. "I know that she doesn't. She loves her cause, and her family more than she will ever love me. But love does not need to be returned to be real, Lorena. And pretending like the love between two people must be equal to matter is foolishness. You should know that."

I blinked. "What the heck does that mean?"

He gave me a sour look. "Do not act so blind."

I frowned harder. "Don't be so vague then. What are you talking about?"

His eyes bored into mine as if they were looking for something. Then his sour look rearranged and he was smiling at me. Then he laughed. "How old are you, Lorena?"

I wasn't even a little sure about why that mattered but I answered him anyway. "I'm nineteen."

He shook his head slowly. "So very young."

I gave his chest a shove. He moved back, but I knew better than to think it was because of my strength. He moved because he wanted to.

"I'm nineteen, dude, not ten. I'm not that young."

"Age and youth are not the same thing. A person can be fifty and still be young, or twelve and know too much of the world. But it takes someone very young to mistake lust for love so easily as you have."

The words were like a punch to my gut. I watched in shocked silence as he wandered away following the now barely visible trail of Dora the swamp hag. If it weren't for Maahes blinking at me halfway between her and us I might not have seen the trail at all. Zane's broad back was a shadow in the mist.

"Hey!" I called, charging after him, clamoring between roots and branches to do it. "Don't you walk away after saying something like that. This isn't some stupid TV show where we can cut to black after some zinger has been delivered. What do you mean?"

He shrugged his shoulders, but his lips were twisted into an amused grin. "I mean exactly what I said Lorena. Lust and love are not the same thing. I had assumed you knew that."

"I love Wei."

"Do you?" His words were light, twisting them into mock sympathy.

I resisted the urge to punch him in the shoulder or something equally futile. "Wei is...he's awesome."

Zane nodded. "My brother is both honorable and loyal. There is no better person in the world. But I do not think that you love him."

The ground was soggy beneath my boots, and my steps were so hard that I was leaving deep grooves in my wake that filled with murky, foul smelling water but that's not why I wrinkled my nose. "What would you know?"

"I watched you, Lorena. I watched you with him every night that I could. More than you realize. I can be a shadow after all. I saw how you two interacted with one another. There is a great deal of lust there. You two can hardly keep your hands to yourselves. It's why he was stolen away. The Order couldn't trust you to wait to fall in love before you," he paused before saying, "enjoyed him."

The blush that rushed to my cheeks was enough to make my head feel light. "First and foremost, the fact that you saw us get...handsy with one another is nothing short of creepy. Just throwing that out there. And secondly, I can love someone and lust after them. They aren't mutually exclusive. Would I be on this quest to get him back if I didn't love him?"

He smirked. "The average person? No. They wouldn't. They would talk themselves out of it a thousand times before they got to their destination. But you have a broad streak of resolve, Lorena. I think it could have been Vlad himself locked up by the Order and you still would have gone after him because you cannot let those around you suffer." He shook his head. "That's kindness, not love. Love is trust, respect, and friendship all rolled up into one."

I frowned. Was he right? Maybe a little. But not about Wei. I loved Wei. I was sure of that. I trusted him. He was easy to trust. And I had respected him from day two.

"I care about him," I finally said. "I trust him."

He nodded. "You might. But that's not love. He loves you but that's not the same."

Whatever I might have said next was interrupted by Dora giving a shout of glee. "Hah! Here he is, here he is. I knew I had not lost him." She started humming again, her spindly hips swishing as she approached what looked like three willow trees woven together. The swamp water was exceptionally low here, and the ground was merely wet rather than soggy. The long slender branches wrapped around what looked, at first, like a cocoon. She tugged at them until they slithered apart to reveal what looked like a long, smoky white crystal with a man trapped inside.

He was an older man, old enough to be my grandfather. His hair had more salt than pepper and was thin enough that it was nearly lost in the bright white of crystal that entrapped him.

"Who is he?" I asked.

"Marco," she said fondly running a hand over the face of the crystal as if she could touch the man beneath. "We were friends once, you know, dear friends. He came to see me. Foolish of him. He got caught up in a spell anyway." She gave the crystal a pat. "Well, he's all yours."

"Once you free him he is."

She frowned. "Was that part of the bargain?"

"Yes," I said. "Yes, it is. You said you'd give me someone who could help me learn."

She gave a bark of laughter. "Well I'm giving him to you. I can't free him. I never said that I would."

"Hey now-"

Her face was filled with an emotion I couldn't place. There was a brightness to her eyes that I didn't understand. It looked similar to a dog's look, when their favorite person picked up their favorite play toy, but I was not her favorite, and she was wasn't a dog. She moved to the very top of the mound we all stood on. Her feet so light she barely displaced the grass. What the heck was she even made of?

Zane was suddenly in front of me. His skin had gone darker, taking on the hint of shadow. "Stay back."

I took a step away. "What are we supposed to do with him?"

She waved her hand flippantly. "I don't care. Just leave, leave and keep your end of the bargain, let me go. Free me."

I shook my head. "I can't use him like that. Not trapped in a crystal."

Her eyes twinkled and went wide with mock shock. "You would break our bargain."

"You broke it first, you lured me here under false pretenses. I can't do anything with that." I waved my hand the length of the crystal. "You lied to me."

Her eyes took on a lethal shine and a ripple of fear swam through me. "I do not lie," she repeated herself, "not once had a lie ever left my lips. What reason would I have for that when the truth is terrible enough?"

A mighty howl broke through the everlasting night. Goosebumps erupted on my flesh, making my skin itch. I took another step back. I got the feeling that something was very, very wrong.

"Lorena, run," Zane said it so softly at first, so flatly that I couldn't make sense of the word. "Lorena!"

"Come to me my love! My Green Man! I've brought something good for you to eat." She sang it like a nursery rhyme, continuing to waggle her nonexistent hips.

My legs prepared to run but I couldn't make them do it. They felt almost hot with the desire to move but I was frozen in place. Another howl ripped through the night and I couldn't move an eyelash, much less my legs.

The barely soggy ground spread apart. The trees shifted as if to make way for what was coming from beneath. Zane shoved at my shoulder and I knew I should be running but fear kept me pinned in place.

A massive shape made of mossy green fur crawled out from the ground. Muck and branches clung to its body as two clawed paws heaved an enormous bulk up. It was a massive shape, and after my eyes adjusted to the fear pounding behind them I realized that this was where the smell of wet dog was coming from. The beast was decidedly lupine, with a long nose and paw-like hands and feet, but the body had a man's shape, and when it finally stood it stood on two legs, not four. His eyes, black as obsidian, stared down at us and it began to drool.

"RUN!" Zane cried, shoving me hard again.

I ran. Something broke inside of me and I ran blindly into the swamp, disrupting frogs and snakes as I went. Maahes launched himself after me. Water splashed around my boots and I fell at least twice that I could remember. It was probably more. I didn't care. It wasn't just that the creature looked so inhuman, it had been the look of hunger in its eyes when it looked at me and Zane, as if we were the top shelf kibble.

When I fell the third time, I chanced a look over my shoulder. I expected to see Zane right behind me, but he wasn't. He hadn't followed me at all. I blinked my confusion. Where was he? What was he doing? A brief touch to the magical line between us told me that he had stayed behind, he was going to fight the beast.

I should let him fight it. I should run. These were my first thoughts, but I shook them away. Zane wouldn't be in this place if it hadn't been for me. I wasn't going to leave him behind now. I just didn't have that in me.

I turned and charged back across the wild path I had made. When I got to the triple tree clearing, Zane was pinned to the ground by the Green Man and Dora was kneeling over him, drawing her claws down Zane's chest, opening him up like he was a package. His skin split. His head thrown back like in a silent scream. Why wasn't he turning into mist? Her eyes were bright with pleasure. She lifted one hand, coated in Zane's blood, and brought it to the creature's lips. The beast licked it off with dog like delight.

Ew. Gross. Not cool. What was wrong with these people? Okay, scratch that, I knew what was wrong. They were all kinds of magically screwed up. Well that ended right now.

"Hey!" I cried out. "Back off my vampire!"

I shoved my magic into Zane like a fist. It was easier this time, as if my magic knew him. It spilled through him, over him, into him. With one mighty shove of obsidian the Green Man went tumbling across the clearing, landing in the swamp with a wet slap.

Dora whirled on me, her teeth drawn back to reveal brown and yellow teeth inside of her mouth. "How dare you!"

"Woman, you started this!" I snapped back.

But she wasn't listening. Instead she launched herself at me, her willowy body slammed into me with more strength than I would have given her credit for. I didn't care. I tumbled with her to the ground, my robes tangling around my legs. She tried to hit me, but the magic that lived in the fabric flared and all she got in was a muted slap. My cheek would grow red, but nothing more. She tried again, her clawed hand nearly shimmering with magic but the same thing happened.

While she was busy glaring at me I shoved my hand into one of the pouches. I came up with a fistful of salt. Salt was the great magic compensator. It was the base to our acid. I threw it in her face and she howled. I rolled, tumbling her off me. She grabbed my leg and jerked, and I slid across the ground.

My training with Wei kicked in. My muscles responded to her attempts to stroke at me before my brain could follow what was happening. I went to some cool place in my head where I was almost watching us fight rather than being a part of it. My arms blocked, my fists struck and I used her strength against her. I could hear Zane fighting in the background, but I couldn't pay attention to it. I had my own battle to win.

Dora shrieked at me, that brittle branch against branch sound echoed in my ears, but it sounded far more human than it had before. I looked at her, and all the places where the salt had brushed were fleshy. She had been pretty once, I realized, with dainty feminine features and sun-tanned skin. Her hair was golden brown, not green, and rich with curls. She swept out at me, but her arm was still broken with Zane's earlier attack and it was nothing. The other one was flesh. It slapped against me, but she didn't have the same training I did. I blocked it.

"Free him!" I grabbed her flesh

"I can't!" she growled.

"Bull." I grabbed her by her now human hair. "You made an entire dream world. There is no way you can't free one witch from magic."

She hissed at me, scrapped a hand down my arm. But in the end, we both knew I had won.

"Call off your beast and free the mage." I gave her a shake.

She spoke in a language I didn't know, but it sounded vaguely Celtic in nature. I didn't know enough of any form of Gaelic to say which it might have been, but the Green Man came to a halt, turning to face his mistress with disappointed eyes. Zane sagged to the ground. He looked tired. He felt tired.

"I do not know if I can do what you ask."

"Well you are going to try." I said, refusing to release her. I understood Zane's resistance to letting her go earlier.

She hesitated. "It will take time."

"We are in a pocket dimension," I said, recalling what she'd told me earlier about having all the time in the world when in such a space. "We've got nothing but time."

~~

Zane was pretty badly injured. He managed to fumble his way to Dora's hut, carrying the big crystalline witch in his arms, but I had to steadily feed him magic to do it. If I was being honest with myself, something I didn't like to do, I wasn't going to be able to keep it up. My magic was like a well, and it was starting to run dry.

We arrived at a hut, barely more than a shack, in the middle of nowhere. It had a single room and a sagging roof. One side of the hut was taking up by a large cooking area, complete with a big cauldron hanging on a swinging arm over a long cold fire. A small bed took up the other side of the room, piled high with patchwork quilts. The whole place smelled like herbs and must.

Dora stoked the fire, and the warm blaze pushed away the bad smells and the dank cold. She pushed food into my hands, and surprisingly it looked good. Sure, it was just bread, sausage, and cheese, but it wasn't covered in muck or mold which made it the most appealing thing that I had seen in the entire swamp.

"Eat," she told me flatly. "I must gather herbs."

"You are leaving?" I said, feeling automatically defensive. I didn't trust her to return.

"I do not have what I need at the hut, and your feet will not do well in my swamp. Rest, and I will return."

Zane was too weak to argue, I was too tired to argue. I watched her go without saying anything else. I sighed. Some heroine I was. I needed to eat, sleep, and regain my energy. Real heroes just kept going even when things sucked. I failed. With that happy thought, I took a bite of bread I hoped wasn't poisoned or enchanted and plopped down on the bed. It was more comfortable than I would have expected.

Zane continued to stand in the doorway, looking like a pale shadow of himself. I scooted over and patted the spot next to me. It was apparently enough of a command that he flopped, face first, on the bed.

His nice clothes were ruined, and he was limp with exhaustion. I felt a wave of sympathy and patted his shoulder.

"I'd offer you some of the food, but vampires don't gain anything by eating."

There was a long bout of silence. "I need blood."

I paused. Then I took another bite and held my arm out to him. He turned his head towards the skin, then looked up at me with golden eyes.

"You would let me feed from you?"

I shrugged. "I have discovered that I have absolutely no problem with being a meal for bloodsuckers. Maybe other people do, but I don't mind. Besides, you are currently connected to me. The very least I can do is open up a vein for you."

He gave me a look so blank of expression that I knew he was being careful. I could have pushed, with words or magic, but I decided not to. Instead I just gave him a smile. "Limited time offer, my friend."

It wasn't the first time that I would feed a vampire, that honor went to Wei. I almost shivered at the memory of it. I don't know if it's me, or vampires, but being bitten felt really good. Like...two hours' worth of hot and heavy make out session good.

"You are thinking of him again." Zane's lips brushed against my inner wrist as he spoke. This time I did shiver.

"Sorry. Can't help it."

"It's....it's alright."

I gave Zane a look. But he wasn't looking up at me, He was looking at my arm. I had pale skin. Both of my parents are some form of European, so my skin is naturally fair. It didn't help anything that all of my hobbies were indoor hobbies. I never got much sun. You could follow the veins in my arm all the way up to my neck. Zane's eyes were doing that. I became very aware of how blue they looked beneath my skin. His brown fingers gently cupped my arm, one around my wrist, one just above my elbow. He laid a kiss against the flesh.

"Dude," I said.

"Forgive me," he whispered. "It has been a long time since a woman has offered her flesh to me."

I raised my brow. "Connie doesn't...."

He shook his head slowly. "No, she does not."

I wasn't sure why that made me feel good, but it did. Perfect Connie, so focused on her quest to screw me over that she wouldn't even offer her blood to the vampire who loved her. I tried to push that down. It wasn't fair to think it, but I did anyway. Oops.

His fangs slid out slowly, and they pricked against my skin. The graze made me gasp. He looked up at me, and his eyes were shimmering gold.

"You...like this..." he had to speak carefully around the fangs.

I took a deep breath. "Yeah, I do."

This time it was him that shivered. I liked seeing him shiver. Jeez. What was wrong with me? Wasn't I in love with someone else? Didn't I love Wei? Of course, I did. I had to. Wei was perfect. I could trust him. I didn't trust Zane. I didn't even get along with Zane...right? Okay, not true. Right up until I realized he was a backstabber I had gotten along with him just fine.

He bit and I gasped, but he didn't pull away. The fullness of his lips was vivid against my skin as he drank me down. My fist clenched and unclenched as waves of pleasure shivered through my body. Parts of me that didn't get nearly enough attention tingled and I had to resist the urge to ask him to do more.

He drank from me. His eyes closed and he took deep swallows from my skin. The connection that existed between us blossomed and I could see exactly what else he wanted to do. A blush surged to my cheeks as his thoughts invaded my own. Zane was...creative.

"Oh," I gasped.

His eyes flashed open and he jerked suddenly away. Two lines of blood trickled down my wrist, but it wasn't as much as it could have been. I felt a little light headed, but I didn't think it was just the fault of blood loss.

"Forgive me," he blurted out, his fangs still bright against his lips.

I shook my head. "Dude, you do not need to say you are sorry for that."

He gave me a long look. "You don't...you aren't...upset?"

I laughed. "Why the heck would I be upset?"

His head tilted to the side. He was definitely feeling better. His color was better, not half so gray. His eyes didn't have the sunken and weary look anymore. I however, definitely needed to eat, and probably take a nap. Yeah, a nap was a fantastic idea.

I ripped off a chunk of bread, wrapped it around on of the sausages and a bit of cheese. He was still looking at me when I took a bite of my slap-dash sandwich.

"You aren't offended?"

I knitted my brows. "I just got a glimpse of your really vivid fantasy of being a human sandwich between you and Wei. That is, in my opinion, the coolest fantasy ever and I am pretty much the exact opposite of offended."

It had been seriously vivid. I hadn't known that a dude would be okay with that kind of pairing, but I had seen it with...well...not my own two eyes, but it was pretty close.

The blush on his cheeks was so dark it was nearly purple. "You are blunt."

I shrugged and took another bite. I could almost feel my body breaking down the food. "Let's be honest here. Blunt gets things said. Some people are super polite, beat around the bush types, I don't have time for that. I liked what you thought, I've said so. What more do you want?"

He paused. "Connie...does not like to be touched."

Okay, while I did appreciate the honesty, that was probably way more about my half-sister than I ever needed to know. Even so, I felt sympathetic. "I'm sorry." I thought of Reikah. "Is she asexual? Sex repulsed?"

He gave me a look like he didn't understand my phrases.

"There are some people who are really adverse to sex. There is a whole spectrum of it, but some of them are sex repulsed. They aren't just neutral about sex, they are turned off. It's no big deal." I shrugged. I was of the opinion that everyone needed to find out who and what they were. I had recently found out that I liked being a vampire snack and was totally cool with being a buffet for two. Neat.

He thought it over. "I don't know what she is. We don't talk about it."

I finished off my food. "What do you talk about?"

"Her quest, the order."

"Sounds like she likes to dominate the conversation." I couldn't help but feel a little petty about that. If Connie wasn't down for naughty time, that was cool, but only talking about the things that interested you wasn't what I would call a nice thing.

"She is driven."

I nodded and laid down on the bed. "Yeah, I know."

He went quiet and I closed my eyes. I seriously needed a nap.

"If I go to sleep you won't kill me, will you?"

I was surprised when I felt him lay down in front of me. It took me a moment to realize he had put himself between me and the door, the only way into the little hut.

"No," he said, "I won't kill you."

I believed him. Shock and amazement.

CHAPTER TEN

By the time I woke up, the other witch was free. I was a little disappointed that I hadn't gotten to see the ritual, but I think that Dora the swamp witch was playing things smart. She had not only freed Marco, as he introduced himself, but she had made herself scarce. All I had of hers was a note scrawled onto paper so old it cracked beneath my fingers and a small clay pot filled with a dark green substance. The note said that by using the substance to draw a symbol of awakening on the crystal I could wake up all the witches, and since she had fulfilled more than her part of the bargain I now owed her.

"A lie never passes her lips, my right foot," I growled as I shoved my feet into my boots.

Zane had left the bed as soon as I started to wake. I knew, thanks to our connection, that he hadn't slept the entire time that I was asleep. I also knew that he had a lot of time to think about things while I had been zonked out. Considering the dreams that I had while I was zonked out...I was pretty sure he was thinking about me, about Wei, and his own feelings. The dreams had not been all bad. Private, yes, but not bad.

I shoved my feet into my boots and stepped out of the hut. Marco and Zane were sharing a quiet conversation.

Marco, who Dora had called The Frenchman, was a very tall man. He stood somewhere around six foot three and had broad shoulders and worn hands. His dull ash hair had been brushed, and carefully styled. It said something to me that he had also washed the clothes that he wore while I had slept.

He turned to me and bowed his head. "It seems that I have you to thank for my return to living."

I had heard a native French accent before. Alan and Genevieve were both born in the French countryside. Marco's had a tinge of something else. I think he was born in Louisiana, not France.

"I'd accept your gratitude, but I have to be honest, I was a little selfish about it." I offered my hand. He took it and pressed his lips to the knuckles. I smirked. Yeah, there was definitely something French about him. It wasn't a flirtatious kiss, but it was romantic. I'm not sure I can explain the difference. "I'm a necromancer too."

He nodded, releasing my hand. "So, Zane has told me. I am impressed with what you have done despite your minimal training."

"You are?" I asked, a small bit of hope kindling in my chest.

"You have learned how to bind the unliving, how to offer them your essence. You have a ghostly familiar who protects you. It took me years of practice to do the same."

I blushed. I couldn't remember the last time someone said I had done something well. It brought a relief I hadn't expected. "Thanks."

He nodded. "When we have more time, I would be happy to teach you more, but I am told that there is a prophecy, and that your intended has been taken from you."

I gave Zane a look. He had been chatty. He gave me an unrepentant shrug. "You were asleep, and I assumed you would tell him when you woke."

He wasn't wrong. "Yeah, we need to free the other witches. They are locked in pocket dimensions...I'm sure Zane filled you in."

Marco gave a brisk nod. "That he did. Are you ready?"

I nodded. "As ready as I can be."

Maahes twirled around my legs as if to tell me that he too was ready. I reached down and gave his ghostly head a scratch.

"Then let us be off."

I'd like to tell you that waking the other witches was a long and arduous thing. It should have been, but it wasn't. Most of the other pocket dimensions weren't nearly as hazardous as Dora's. In fact, almost all of them were inviting in their own ways. Some were small cottages in the middle of perfect spring time forests. Some were houses by the beach, propped up on large stilts so that the waves could crash around them. Some were mountain cabins, piled with snow. Others weren't even earthly in their splendor. One of them was a fairy tale castle in the clouds, with wispy servants to attend to our every need. I was really hoping that I could craft the best pocket dimension ever when I got powerful enough.

The witches were as varied as the domains they lorded over, or were visiting, depending. Some were old, some were young, they were every gender, race, and affiliation. One was deaf, a few were missing limbs, I had never seen the better part of a hundred people define diversity so well.

Most of the witches were willing to hear us out, some had already heard from Marquessa, some hadn't. But in the end, I had a steadily building army. After all, a lot of them really wanted magic back, and when they had heard that I had bested Dora the Swamp Witch, they were even more willing to join up with me. I was a little vague about the fact that she had gotten away, but that was a truth for another day.

I had all the witches who wanted to join me go down into Marquessa's house. They could eat or rest or whatever they needed. That was all on them. Marco promised to watch over them, organize them. He seemed dependable, if a little aloof.

Jenny, Marquessa, and Reikah were stuck in a pocket dimension that looked like a mansion. Not like the vampire mansion, but a California one, tucked between mountains and an ocean with a big blue pool taking up the backside of it. I expected a Hollywood starlet to own it, and if I was being honest, I wasn't let down.

"There they are!" I said, charging out the sliding glass door towards the pool, and the lounge chairs that were there.

"I'll stay here," Zane said, waving at me from the doorway. Apparently, the fake California sun was still too real for his vampire skin. I nodded and went to rescue my friends.

Jenny was wearing a golden bathing suit. Her nails had been painted to match. Reikah who was perched on a seat next to her, wore a long red sarong dress, her hair pulled up into a messy bun. If they weren't trapped in crystal they would have looked like an attractive couple enjoying a day at the pool. Marquessa wore pale coral cotton slacks and a sleeveless top, showing off her arms. She was looking up at the sky, her face frozen in consternation.

It was the last woman who I was struck by. She looked like a bombshell, you know, those vixens from the silver screen. Her hair was carefully coiffed, and the one piece she wore managed to look sultry and demure all at once. She had a tiny mole by her nose, and her hands were thrown up in the air as if reaching for the sky.

What was it Dora had said? Marquessa had found a witch who could bring them all together? I didn't know how, but I was sure I was going to get my answer soon.

I took the last of the goop inside the clay pot and smeared it over each surface in the now familiar symbol of awakening.

I don't know if you've ever seen crystal melt, but that's what this looked like. A shimmer swept across the flat surface, and it slipped away like snow in the sunlight. For a moment, the witches all stayed exactly as they were, and then took their first breath in who knew how long.

Marquessa looked at me, confusion knitting her brows. "Lorena? How did you get here?"

"Lorena!" Jenny jumped up and threw her arms around me. She smelled like coconut oil. I hugged her back. "Sweetie, what happened?"

"Oh god, where do I even start?"

"Is this her?" a breathy voice worthy of Marilyn Monroe cut in. "She looks...young."

I turned my head and took in the Hollywood vixen. Frozen she'd been pin-up worthy, in motion she was glorious. She gave me a red lipped smile and I blushed. I wasn't sure what it was, but I felt my entire face go cherry tomato red. She laughed.

"Oh, she's old enough." She gave me a wink. I shook my head.

"What?"

"Stop it, Margot." Marquessa said lightly.

Margot gave a little shrug of her shoulders, which were a shade of peaches and cream despite her sunny residence. "It's habit."

"Margot is part fae," Jenny said with a roll of her arms, one dark arm still slung around me. "She has...charms."

Reikah rolled her eyes, her lips set into a jealous line. Even so she shot me a grin. "I'm happy you are alright. We worried about you."

"Yeah," Jenny said, giving me a little shake. "Are you finally ready to join the world of the living? Last time I called you were...well...zombified."

I must have been pretty bad off since I didn't even remember that. "I'm okay. I'm ready to go get Wei back."

The women shared a look.

"Back?" Marquessa said. "Lorena..."

I held up a hand. I already knew what she was going to say. On the bright side, I had gotten a lot of practice telling my story to people who were out of the loop. It took the better part of an hour, and somewhere during my tale of woe and misery Margot the part fae had pushed a drink that tasted of ice and fruit into my hand. I sipped it in between stories of mathemagics, vampires, and swamp witches. *Oh my, it had been a heck of a few days.*

"So in the end, Wei isn't dead, and I am going to go save him," I finished, taking the last sip of the drink.

"Well, that's some story," Margot said cheerfully. I wasn't sure that she knew how to be anything but cheerful. Her long legs crossed and uncrossed. "I cannot wait to see how it all turns out."

Marquessa was quiet. "You have already contacted the others?"

"You guys were in the last room" I said. "Everyone else is awake. Marco is making sure they are prepared."

Marquessa nodded her approval. "Marco was in the military once, long ago. He'll get them ready. But will you be ready?" she asked.

All of their eyes looked towards me. It wasn't an easy question and it weighed on my shoulders. Was I ready? Well, I mean, I'd prefer a lot more time to level grinding, gear up, get everything together, but the fact was I didn't know what the Order had planned, and I didn't even know if Wei was still alive. I hoped so. The thought of him being gone was enough to make my whole chest ache.

"Let's do this."

Marquessa and Margot headed out of the pocket dimension to join the others, leaving me with Reikah and Jenny.

"I can draw a map of the temple," Reikah said.

I nodded. "Take Zane with you. He might know things you don't and visa versa or whatever."

She gave me a dubious look. "Zane?"

I nodded. "Yeah, I know. But he's been...helpful."

There was a low flutter in my stomach when I remembered how he had protected me at the swamp. I tried to ignore it. I wasn't the kind of girl who gave her affections so easily, right? Crap. Maybe I was. This voyage of self-discovery was filled with way too much truth. I needed a vacation. I kinda wished I could stay by the pool.

"If you say so." Reikah reached a hand out to Jenny who squeezed it affectionately, and then Reikah left the two of us alone.

"Okay," Jenny said, plopping down on the lounge. She crossed her long legs and looked up at me. "Be honest, how are you feeling?"

I plopped down next to her. "About what part?"

"Let's start with attacking this temple."

I took a deep breath. "Honestly? I'm okay with that. I want to do that. I am ready to charge in there Rambo style and go kickboxing rampage on their butts. Jackie Chan style or something."

Jenny laughed and gave me a bump with her shoulder. "And the prophecy? What are you going to do about that?"

That was a far more difficult question and it took me a long time to think it over. "Zane says I don't love Wei, that I just lust after him. I think he might be right, just a little. I hate that."

"That you don't love Wei? Or that Zane's right about something?"

"Both," I admitted, dragging one hand down my face. "This whole time I told myself that I needed to be in love before I would take someone to my bed. I have almost dragged Wei to my bed twice and honestly? If I hadn't been so sure that Zane liked my sister I might have taken him too."

"So, you like them both?" she asked gently.

"Does that make me a terrible person?" I blurted.

"No, it doesn't. Your heart isn't a pie, Lorena, it's not chopped up and handed out in slices. For some people there is only one perfect person for them, for others? Well, it's not that cut and dry. Some people have a lot of love to give, and can give it to two or more without a problem."

I gave her a look that was filled with my self-doubt. "Sounds slutty to me."

"Don't hate," Jenny said, laying back beneath the perfect sun. "Sluts get to have lots of fun, it's the rest of the world that makes it hard on them. And you know what? If you want my honest opinion."

"When have you ever given me anything else?" I teased.

She gave me a grin worthy of a magazine. "If you are going to imbue the world with magic? You might need more than one lover to get it done."

I blushed all the way up to the roots of my hair. Jeez, what was it with these past few days? I was either blushing or crying. It was beginning to make me worry about myself. Not really, but a little bit. "Sure, I'll just tell the vampire boys, 'sorry guys, my decision is to pick these two'."

She shrugged. "Why not?"

I shook my head, not even willing to go over the why or why nots. "Come on, let's go assault a temple."

"You always take me to the nicest places."

CHAPTER ELEVEN

Before we left I had one final thing to take care of. Marco, Zane, Jenny, Reikah and myself drove up to the mansion. It was just past dusk and the dim lights were burning. The door opened before I could knock. Yasmina stood there looking like a ferocious, barely tamed animal still in human form.

"You," she hissed.

"Yup," I said, "big bad me. The one who kicked your butt, is here."

"You still can't have him." Her lips pulled back to show her teeth, already going sharp. Gee-zus, someone needed to get this girl into some anger management therapy. I had never seen her be anything but pissed off, and usually at me.

"Still don't want him." I said. "But I'm not here for that."

"Then what are you here for?"

Just hearing Vlad's voice made my skin crawl. It was good to know that I wasn't attracted to every male vampire. Just most of them. Go me.

Vlad materialized out of the darkness in the same way that I assumed Zane could do. Dark tendrils of smoke coiled together to create a vampire out of pretty much nothing. Vlad formed a moment latter, wearing a blood red top with frills around the neck and cuffs, a long black jacket, and pants that looked nearly painted on. He should have looked horrible, but he made it work. He kept a safe distance away from me. He was wary, I liked it.

"We are going to assault the temple, I'd like the help you and the rest of the vampires. Then I am going to fulfill the prophecy."

He raised his brow. "You will accept my offer?"

"I didn't say I was going to do it with you," I pointed out. "But here's the thing. I want magic in this world. I want it more than I can tell you. Ever since I was a kid I wanted to live in a world with dragons, and vampires and everything else. Blame it on the video games, or the comic books, or whatever you want to. I wanted it so bad that I used to cry about it. I dunno, make of that what you will. You aren't my therapist. But we are going to attack the Temple, and all of you are invited to join us."

"And what will you offer me?"

I laughed, and even to me it sounded derisive. "Dude, I'm going to be giving you back the ability to create more vampires. At the end of all of this? You will owe me."

A hand curled over his arm. Anja stood there with her wise dark eyes. She reached up and tucked his collar around his neck. It was a wifely motion, an affectionate one. He turned his gaze on her, and they shared a silent conversation. A moment later he bowed his head.

"We will join you."

"Good," I said. "Then pack up."

"You will make war now?"

I shrugged. "I've put this off long enough, and I don't know how much time Wei still has. Let's go make a battle plan."

~~

It sounded like the beginning of a really bad joke. The witches, the vampires, and a prophecy girl approached the temple at midnight. A year ago, I would have thought it was a joke, but today? It was just my life choices.

I had traded in the ruined robes of my grandmother for a tank top and a leather jacket. My dad had inscribed mathematical symbols into the jacket to protect me. I liked it. It went better with my boots. He'd done the same for a pair of wristlets he'd found, wearing them made me feel kinda like Wonder Woman. What more could a girl want in life?

There were a little over a hundred of us. Witches from every walk of life, dressed in every style of clothing a person could imagine, all shoulder to shoulder with one intent in mind. To help me take back the magic that they had lost, or had never been able to gain. The vampires were a dark shadow, save for Genevieve and Alan, who both looked like angels. They formed a semi-circle around Marco and I, and my magic was so ready that it itched at my skin. My dad stood just behind them, he hadn't been willing to stay behind this time. I wasn't going to tell him no. This was his fight too.

The temple looked more like a fortress, but I expected no less from the Order of the Loyal Hermit. It was all gray stone and barbed wire. The wire had been formed into symbols, I didn't know them, but I knew that they were protective in nature. It took Reikah, and her knowledge of the Order, and my dad, with his knowledge of inscription to take it down.

Before they were done a blast of sound hit our gathering. It was so loud and so unexpected that nearly all of us crumpled to our knees. All save for the deaf witch. She looked around at us and understanding crossed her features. She threw one hand into the air, and a moment later the sound dissipated. By the time that had happened, however, faces appeared at small slit windows around the temple.

"Margot," I called.

"Best to look away," Margot smirked.

I had not understood the term "charming" before Margot. It was hard not to look at her, it was harder still to look. Her robes were a flutter of golden silk. It brought out the warmth in her skin, making her look softly pink. She laughed, and the sound rolled over the crowd.

Then she began to sing. I didn't know the song, it was in a language I'd never heard, but it made me think of all the things that I wanted. I wanted Wei back, safe and happy. I wanted my dad to not worry about me anymore. I wanted Jenny and Reikah to live a long life together. I wanted the child that everyone told me was going to bring magic into the world. I wanted Zane to get over my sister. I wanted so many things...

A pair of hands clapped over my ears and I found myself looking up into big golden eyes. They were so bright, and so easy to give into. Zane's eyes.

"Stay here," he said, "a Siren's song is not easy to ignore."

I blinked, and now that I knew what it was, it didn't have nearly as much effect on me. I shook my head and gave his lips a light kiss. I don't know who was more surprised him or me.

"What was that for?" he asked.

I shrugged. "Maybe you'll second guess yourself before the inevitable betrayal." I gave his cheek a pat. "This probably is the worst possible moment for this, but I gotta say, I don't think you love my sister."

He frowned at me. "Is this another tactic to assuage me?"

I don't know if I actually understood what the word assuage meant, but I was going to guess it meant "turn."

"No," I said, "You can love someone who doesn't love you back, that's fine. But I don't think you can love someone who doesn't even respect you."

He gave me a look, and I didn't need the tether that still held us together to know that he was angry with me. He could be angry. Hard truths pissed a lot of people off. But we could deal with that later.

The front doors were opening on the temple, and a slew of people clad in gray robes were coming out. Their arms stretched out as they tried to get to Margot.

That's when the first volley went over. Spells of every variety slammed across the wide expanse between us and them. People flew backwards, and the Siren spell was broken.

"Go!" Marquessa called out. "It's your time!"

I wasn't part of the main attack force. The plan had been fairly simple, and Vlad had been the one to come up with it. I guess all those years in the military had been helpful.

The hardest part about getting into the temple was the fact that it was so closed off. It was right up against a mountain which meant there was only one direction that we could come from. The front. So we had to draw the cult out, and there was no better way to do that than Margot. Now that that was done, and the doors were wide open, Me, Zane, Alan, Dmitri, and Genevieve were going inside. This way both necromancers had some vampires with them.

Jenny had wanted to come, but I needed her with the main forces. Her stone magics were much better on large forces than smaller ones. An opinion made valid by the way the bedrock shook beneath us, scattering group of cultists as me and my coterie of undead charged inside.

"Okay, Maahes," I said, "let's find Wei."

The inside of the temple was as gray and lifeless as the outside. Jeez. What was it about these people and their monochrome color scheme? I followed the tabby cat as he went around from room to room, looking for the vampire that he liked best.

I knew something was wrong when my tabby cat froze. Maahes wasn't your normal cat, what with him being dead and all, but he wasn't prone to going vampire still either. I held up a hand and before I could say anything Maahes was dragged across the ground, towards a room that seemed like it was more central to the temple than not. He howled in feline pain.

"Maahes!" I screamed, charging after him. I was dimly aware that the vampires were following me.

I didn't know that a ghost could feel pain, but I felt Maahes. His claws dug into the concrete, and he struggled to keep from whatever was pulling him down the corridor. His eyes were big in his head and his stripped tail was poofed out.

He disappeared through a door, and it took me one terrified kick to charge in after him. No one hurt my kitty.

I came to a halt just inside the door. There was a short set of stairs that gave us just enough room to gather on.

The room was massive. Like, half a football field large. It was a perfect octagon, and looked more like a temple than anything else that I had seen in this fortress. Nine-foot-tall pillars, Greek in style, held up the ceiling. The ground was made of black marble, so shiny and perfect that I could see myself reflected in it.

And in the very center stood Connie. She was wearing her gray robes, but the hood was pulled back so that I could see her freckled face. It had been a long time since I had seen her in the flesh. We were the same height, and had similar builds, but that was about where the similarities stopped. Her hair was a riot of curls, in shades of red and blonde. She had constellations of freckles across her face, neck and arms. She carried a pot in her arms, as long as her torso, and her eyes were filled with disgust.

"So it's true," she sneered. "You are a necromancer."

I blinked. Really? That's what she was going to open with? "Well, yeah," I said. "You got a problem with that?"

Her sneer deepened. "The undead are lesser creatures."

"Whoa."

"Connie," Zane's voice was breathy and strangled.

She looked at him, almost as if she had just realized he was there. I don't know what I expected to see. If it had been mean I'd have apologized for saying something like that. She barely bothered to give him a millisecond of her attention before she turned back to me.

"I should have known you'd be so pathetic."

"What the heck." I shook my head. "Okay, we are going to have to school you in rudeness another day. Where is Wei?"

She laughed, and it was a bitter sound. "By now? Dead. You took too long big sister."

"Liar." I surged forward.

She shrugged. "Even if he's not, by the time I get done with you he will be."

The door slammed shut behind us, locking us in the room. I had just long enough to muse over the concept of epic boss battle before she lifted the jug over her head and poured it out. It was blood, and it sloshed over her Carrie style. Gross.

She threw her arms into the air and a hundred symbols that I hadn't seen flared to life. They were carved into every available surface, the floor, the walls, the pillars. Even the ceiling was blanketed in them. I recognized plenty of them, most were summoning magics, some were protective, some talked about beasts and stars. But I couldn't put them all together, and by the time I was sure they meant something bad for me, the ground was beginning to warp beneath my feet.

Strong arms hauled me away from the black marble, and back unto the entryway stairs. Dmitri put a protective arm around my middle and hauled me against his chest while Zane, Genevieve, and Alan stepped in front of me. It was strange to feel so protected.

My sister's eyes found mine anyway and we shared a look filled with knives and meaning. Her lips curled into a knife sharp smile and I was reminded a little of Dora, the Swamp Witch. Magic pulsed through the room, beating down around me. It smelled like blood and wood and starlight. The hairs on the back of my neck stood up.

The floor was shifting everywhere but the stairs and the spot where my sister stood.

"Don't do this," I didn't know exactly what she was doing, but I knew it couldn't be good. Magic that required so much blood didn't seem like it could end well.

"Come to me, Beast!"

The floor surged up like a waterfall going the wrong way. I tried to take another step back but Dmitri held me close.

The floor, which looked more like a night sky, wrapped around my sister like a wave, and then it took shape. Four legs, a long powerful body, and head that looked like something between a bear and a pitbull, broad and flat and powerful. Fur grew across its body, rippling like starlit shadows. It threw back its head and howled. It wasn't like an animal's howl. It was like the lowest note on a very long electronic keyboard, with the bass turned all the way up. It made my teeth ache.

It took me a moment to realize what she had done. The creature swam around her protectively. My sister had a talent for beast magic, and blood magic and she had managed to combine the two. She had bonded herself to them. It was a hag's trick.

"You can't do that!" I cried out.

"You would bring magic to everyone!" She snapped back at me. "I will do whatever it takes."

"Connie, please," Zane's deep voice was filled with a plea.

She rolled her eyes in response. "You, you are even more pathetic than she is. What are you hoping? For my love? My attention?" She laughed like it was the worst joke ever. "You are so stupid. Haven't you figured it out yet? I don't love you. You don't love me. My mother magic must have worked way too well."

Zane's face filled with shock. He probably understood what she was saying better than I did. My mom was a mind mage, given enough time she could brainwash them into thinking whatever she wanted them to. Zane had a similar power, but his wasn't so long lasting. One time he told me to relax and it felt like I'd had a ten-hour massage.

"It's...not...real."

Connie sneered. "A vampire isn't capable of love."

Well, that I knew wasn't true. Alan was in love with Dmitri, and Wei was in love with me and there was absolutely no magic involved with any of that. But it was clear by the look on her face that Connie believed it.

"But..." Zane slid to his knees and my heart went out to him, but there was no time to offer comfort now.

"Beast! Get them!"

The creature howled that terrifying howl again and charged at us. I didn't have time to think I threw my power into the vampires and they drank it in. They were already strong and fast, I made them better.

Dmitri jumped in front of me, taking the brunt of the hit. Alan and Genevieve darted to the left and the right, flanking the great creature. Zane was still kneeling on the ground, looking like he had been kicked in the gut.

The fight was too fast for me to follow. Alan and Genevieve took turns lashing at the creature from either side, their claws digging into star speckled fur. It snarled and snapped at them, But Dmitri, who shifted into a beastman himself, was there to take every hit. When he weakened, I threw my magic into him, reinvigorating him, making him like new. We were unstoppable. At least we were until Connie attacked me.

I went tumbling to one side, and she snarled at me.

"You will destroy the world!"

"Nope," I said, even as her blood-soaked hands went around my neck. "Just you."

I hadn't realized how angry I was at her. I had thought that I didn't really care all that much about her doing our mother's bidding...but I was pretty pissed off. I had always wanted a sister, almost as much as I wanted magic, and this one was the worst one that I could even think of. She could have been my friend, she could have stood with me, she could have taken the time to see things from my point of view, but instead she betrayed me and that just hurt so much. Then, the fact that she had known about the magical whammy put on Zane and had taken advantage of it? Man, that just made it worse.

I used my hips to tumble her off me and we crashed down to the steps and onto the marble floor. It was far more solid now, but the blood that had spilled on it made it slick. She threw her hands at me and raw magic sent me flying backwards, slapping into one of the pillars. I was going to have some pretty impressive bruises on my back, that is if I survived long enough to bruise. Life goals.

I threw magic back at her, it wasn't half so strong, since my magic was already being split four ways. It was enough to disrupt her and then I tackled her to the ground and pinned her arms above her head, keeping her from casting spells.

"Why do you hate me so much?" I growled. "What did I ever do to you?"

"You were born."

"Oops," I said, maintaining my title as queen of comebacks.

She tried to get up, but she couldn't, not with me weighing her down.

"We could have been friends."

She gave me a look that told me I was an idiot. "You killed my dad."

She jerked her hands out of my grip, a move made easier by the slick blood, and hit me so hard I saw stars. My head rocked to the side. She kicked me across the jaw and I tumbled back. Then she was on top of me, a blade held high in the air. It had a ribbon like look to it, like a wave, with a periolously sharp tip.

"You killed him!"

"He started it!"

Yeah, I know. I could have said pretty much anything else, but apparently fear of death reverts my brain back to that of a kindergartner. I had killed her dad, and he had started it, but it sounded like a childish excuse even to me.

"Die!" She snarled.

I don't know why I didn't really expect her to kill me until that moment. I think a part of me had been hoping, really hoping, that she'd remember the fun times that we'd had as friends, that she would admit that she too had wanted a sister all these years. But the tip of that dagger glittered in the strange room and it was nothing compared to the vicious light in her eyes. She had every intention of killing me.

"Connie!" I cried out just as she began to swing the blade down.

A dark arm wrapped around her neck and hauled her off of me. She screamed her frustration as the dagger clattered to the floor. My brain was frazzled, surprised I wasn't dead. Zane had her in some sort of hold, his arms beneath hers, his fingers interlocked behind her head. She squirmed and jerked.

"Stop this!" he pleaded with her. His eyes were glittering gold. "Please, Connie."

"Get off of me you undead freak! Don't touch me." Her words dripped with venom. Her teeth were visible between tight, angry lips. She looked like a wounded animal caught in a trap. Her body slithered this way and that as she tried to free herself.

He whipped her around, took her face between his hands. The look he gave her made my heart ache. "Please, Connie. You don't have to do this. I love you."

She laughed, and it was a mean sound. "Didn't you hear me you freak? You don't love me, it's a lie."

"I don't care," he said, leaning down to give her a kiss.

She jerked away from him so hard that she stumbled. He watched her go but he didn't try to go after her. He stood there, his proud shoulders slumping forward, his newly cleaned clothes slathered in blood.

Connie whirled on me. She moved to charge and Zane caught her up again.

"I can't let you hurt her," he said.

She snarled and hissed like a cat. "She must die! Her blood will unmake the world!" She was almost frothing with her rage; every word was spit out like rotten meat. "Do you love me or not?"

Red lines spilled over his cheeks. He was crying bloody tears. "I do."

"Then do what I say! Kill her," she snapped the order as if she expected it to be followed. A line of tension ran through his shoulders and he turned his head away, closing his eyes as if he could unmake everything that was happening.

"I... can't."

She howled her rage, trying to jerk out of his arms. She swung at him, her small pale fists hit at him over and over again, and not once did he try to defend himself. The attacks shouldn't have hurt, but my sister was filled with hag magic, new and untamed. Bruises formed on vampire skin, no easy feat, and I heard ribs crack beneath her tempest of rage.

"Kill her!" she shrieked at him. "If you love me, kill her! If you love me prove it."

A rush of emotions filled me and I knew that they weren't mine. I saw Connie as he saw her. I saw her hooking him up to that machine, promising him that when it was over they would be together. I saw her promising kisses that she would never give. I saw her demanding that he follow me. Each time she made some terrible command of him, she was asking him to prove his love. I saw all these things, and I could feel his hurt and his sorrow. I knew that he hated himself, loathed himself for what he had done, more so now that he knew it was a lie. I knew what needed to be done, but I also knew that he couldn't do it.

The magic that existed between Zane and I hummed. He jerked in response to her command of devotion. My own magic flared. Her blinked and looked up at me.

Vampires would do anything for the person they loved, he had told me once, all they had to do was ask. Apparently, when a mind mage was involved, that was extra true. "Prove it." It was a command phrase, a trigger word for hypnosis. Connie would demand proof of his affections and he would do whatever she demanded. But here I was, with necromantic control over him, interfering with my mother's magics. Oops. My bad.

"No," he said, and he shuddered to say it.

Connie snarled. "What did you just say?"

"No. I said no. I will not kill Lorena. I will not kill her. I will not harm her. I will never raise my hand against her, or those she cares for." His deep baritone voice rumbled with the promise as he took two long strides towards Connie. "I will not lie for you, cheat for you, steal for you. I will not be your weapon, nor will I be your victim."

"You...you cannot do that. My mother...her magic."

"Is nothing compared to the link between necromancer and thrall." He said thrall as if he was almost proud of it. "Your mother's pitiful mental magics can do nothing but make demands of me. Her's," he motioned with a hand in my direction, "can raise me from the near death that you put me in, invigorate me, feed me and empower me. I draw from her, and her from me, and that...that is what love is." He looked at me and I felt my heart skip a beat. He loved me. I didn't need the connection between us to see it, to feel it, but it was there anyway.

"How dare you!" she screamed. "You are mine!"

"Only because I didn't know any better."

She hurled herself at him, wild magic thrummed through the room and swung against him like a hammer. He jerked backwards, tumbled to the floor. Her rage was a palpable thing, beating around the room, and I gotta be honest. I did not understand it. She'd made it clear that she didn't love him...but apparently couldn't handle that he cared about someone else. Ugh.

"Get off him!" I cried out. I picked up the dagger in my hands.

She didn't even acknowledge me. She just brought her magic down on Zane over and over again in a fit of vengeful frustration.

Connie wouldn't stop. She wasn't the swamp witch who just wanted to be left alone. She was a vengeful person, filled with the righteous indignation of the zealot. She believed I would unmake the world, that I would kill everything with magic. She believed it all the way down to her toes. She would kill me, she would kill Zane, and she would feel nothing but happiness in it.

I grabbed her by her riot of curls and hauled her away from Zane. She was stronger than she should have been, all that magic, but I had martial arts training and I sent her a few feet in the direction of away.

"I'm sorry." I said. I think I was mostly talking to Zane, who had seen the dagger in my hand, but a small part of me was talking to that little girl who had dreamed of having a sister all those years ago.

Zane looked at me but he didn't respond.

With a ferocious wail Connie threw herself at me. All I had to do was lift the blade. I killed my sister. Jeez, even now it feels so terrible, even knowing that she would have killed me? It doesn't matter. I didn't have time to mourn what had never been as her body slid to the ground. I didn't even have time to tell Zane that I felt terrible for what I was doing. All I could do was drop the blade and swallow the sick feeling in my throat before a terrible sound reverberated around the room.

"Dimitri!"

Alan's voice didn't sound like his own, but I instantly knew what happened. Dmitri's body was lying prone on the ground. I had been so focused on the fight with Connie that I hadn't been paying attention to the massive beast. It was smaller than it had been, not by much, but it was noticeable. Maybe my sister had been empowering it the same way I empowered vampires. I didn't know. But Dmitri was on the ground, bleeding from at least four places that I could see, and all of them were bad.

Alan's eyes went big and he soared through the air like the angel I always thought him to be. His delicate claws tore into fur and flesh over and over again while bloody tears dripped over his cheeks. I thought I'd have to step in, but before I knew it the animal was dead.

I dashed to Dmitri's side, took his head between my hands. He was fading, I could see it in his eyes.

"I'm sorry," he whispered, his voice thick with the accent of mountains and misty mornings.

"You've done nothing wrong." I brushed his hair from his face.

He laughed, and nearly choked on it. "I hurt you, for that I cannot forgive myself."

"I forgive you," I said, I meant it.

Alan was suddenly there, cursing at him hotly in French. "What have you done, you savage?" he demanded. "You've gotten yourself killed."

"It would have been you," Dmitri whispered back, his voice shades lighter than it should have been. "and you are far too lovely to die."

It was then that I knew that Dmitri was aware of Alan's feelings. Dmitri reached a bloody hand out and touched Alan's cheek. I think he intended to wipe away Alan's tears, but instead he left a smudge of red.

"You can't die," Alan whispered.

No I thought, *he couldn't. I wouldn't let that happen.* Not now. My magic was running low, but I'd have enough, just enough to keep Dmitri going. I pushed a little into him and he gasped.

"No!" He shook his head, but he couldn't resist what my magic could do for him. "You do not know what has happened to Wei."

I shook my head and transferred his weight to Alan, who took him in his arms. Alan looked at me with so much gratitude I knew it was worth it.

"My love isn't the only one that matters," I said simply. "Genevieve, watch over them."

She nodded and pressed a thankful hand to mine. "Be safe, necromancer."

"You too," I said.

As I turned to leave, Zane fell into step beside me. I knew better than to tell him to stay. I didn't need the connection to know that he would follow me, and protect me, wherever I went. I also didn't need it to know that Alan's lips were brushing Dmitri's in a tender kiss. I smiled. Here's hoping we all got a happy ending.

~~

There were a hundred rooms in that blasted temple, and I must have gone through every last one of them looking for Wei. I knew, via the wisdom of video games and comic books, that she would be my final boss. My mother. For all I had wanted a sister in my life, I had wanted a mother too. I had wanted someone to talk to when there had been a boy who caught my interest, when I had cried over a fictional character, when school had been bad. I'd wanted someone capable of telling my dad no, that we weren't moving, and for helping me settle in if we had.

Man, had I drawn the short straw.

But in most of those rooms I found nothing but cultists. I didn't kill any of them. I had the sneaking suspicion that my mother's magic was at work in most of them. It had probably been in my sister too, but I couldn't do anything about that now. Between me, Zane, and magic I managed to knock out or tie up those who, for whatever reason, hadn't joined the main force outside.

My mother hadn't joined them either. I found her in a room that looked like a lab. There was a long silver table, not unlike the one I had found Zane on all those weeks ago, but it was Wei laying on top of it this time.

When I had rescued Zane he had looked too skinny, too lean. Wei looked worse. Twenty IV's were plugged into various parts of his nearly naked body, and I could count every bone in him. His lips were so dry that they were little more than cracked scraps across his teeth, and his eyes were yellowed and sunken. There was a single window in the room, and it was flung open. During the daylight, I bet this whole place was flooded with a gentle light, just enough to burn a vampire slowly.

I didn't even see my mother at first. I was so focused on him. I rushed to his side and I didn't need to see my tears puddling on his skin to know that I was crying for him. "Oh god, Wei....Wei!" I cried out again and again. I was too late. He didn't move beneath my touch, no blood pumped in his veins. I couldn't feel him. I couldn't even sense that essence of undead that I knew so well.

The world went hazy, and my head went light. He was dead. The room was too bright, too hot. I tugged at the IV's, desperate to get them out of his ruined flesh. The skin crackled.

"No, no, no, no," I whispered beneath my breath, as if by saying it I could take back his death. I leaned over him and kissed those cracked lips. My lip caught on one of his vampiric teeth. I didn't care. I kissed him again. True loves kiss was supposed to be magic, right? The thought was so desperate, so wild and yet I still clung to it.

"You are too late," a gentle voice purred.

It was a mother's voice, and I hated her for that. I hated that even now she sounded like everything a mother ought to sound like.

"You killed him,"

"It should have happened weeks ago." She stepped out from behind a desk that I had been to blind with feelings to even notice. She looked like a mother, even now. Her eyes were bright with warmth, her pale hair delicately styled around her face. She looked like she should be on her way to a PTA meeting or a soccer game. Well, if she'd been wearing anything but Cultists robes that is. "He clung to life for a very, very long time."

"You...you killed him," I whispered, still not wholly believing it. I wanted to be angry at her, I wanted to scream and throw things and hit her, but I couldn't bring myself to do anything. I felt heavy, so heavy. It hurt.

"You killed Markus," she spat, her face twisting so suddenly that I took a step back. Her hand swung out and slapped me across the face. An instant later Zane was there, materializing from mist. The next slap was caught in his hand. Her eyes went wide. She hadn't expected him. "Zane?" she gasped. Then realization hit her. "Where is Connie? Where is my daughter?"

It still hurt that she showed such devotion to Connie. Why didn't she love me even half so much? I was just as much her daughter as Connie had been. I opened and closed my mouth several times to tell her what had happened, but no sound came out. Some bad ass heroine I was.

"She is gone," Zane said flatly.

"You...you didn't protect her?"

"No."

"You had to, you had to protect her!"

There was a brief moment of silence. I felt like I should interrupt it, but my brain was still too shocked to form much but the most basic of sentences.

He shook his head. "Your magic isn't so strong as that."

I wish that I could tell you some grand fight happened between me and my mother. It didn't. She shrieked her rage and tried to fight Zane, but it didn't help. Zane was by far stronger, and now that I wasn't keeping three other vampires alive for battle, there was plenty of strength for him. He just held her as she yelled angrily at us both. She tried to pull her mind magics on Zane, but my magic kept that from happening, and wouldn't you know it? His mental magics kept her from doing the same to me. It was a pretty impressive stalemate.

"I hate you," she finally snarled at me, realizing that the battle was over. "I hate you."

I wish it hadn't hurt. I wish I could say that I was stone cold to her insults, but I wasn't. Even now, even after everything I wished that she could find it in herself to love me. It might be pathetic, and even ridiculous but I really wanted her to just relent and say that she loved me, or even liked me, just a little. Instead she spit at me, literally. After all that had happened she puckered up her lips and shot a gob of spittle at me. Gross.

"Real mature," I snarled, wiping my face.

"I should have killed you when that bitch said the prophecy."

"Well, you didn't."

"You've taken everything! You took Markus, you took Connie! You will remake the world with some demon spawn child."

I shrugged. I didn't feel like defending myself against her.

Then she did something I should have seen coming, but didn't. She ripped herself out of Zane's arms and made a mad dash for the window. I felt a wave of shock as she flung herself out of it. It was not the epic boss battle that I had expected. I blinked, pretty sure that my mom had manipulated my brain into just thinking that she was dead, but a brief glance out the window told me otherwise. I will never get that image out of my head, not the guilt I felt at doing absolutely nothing to stop her. Feelings are weird.

I should have felt elated. We had won, the cult was obliterated and wouldn't stand in my way, but all I could do was look at Wei's emaciated body.

"You do love him," Zane said after a moment.

I nodded my head, taking a dead hand in mine, wishing that I could do something, anything to make this better. "I do love him. I think I've loved him since the first cold glare he gave me. But that's...it doesn't matter."

Zane walked past me and picked up the IV's. Before I could ask him what he was doing he jammed them into his skin. An instant later blood, my blood if we wanna get technical about it, started to flow back through the complicated tubing and into Wei.

"What are you doing?" I managed.

"You love him," he said simply. "I can give him to you. I can make amends."

I shook my head, moving to jerk the IV out of his arm. He held me away. I tried again, and he shifted away from me. Let me tell you, it is impossible to catch a vampire who can turn into mist.

"Why?"

He gave me a look. "Because, I love you."

I knew he meant it but I shook my head anyway. In that moment, I knew that I loved him too. Call me whatever you want for being in love with two guys at once, call me fickle, call me names, tell me that I'm an idiot or frivolous or whatever, but I couldn't not love them both. "Zane, I-"

He held up one hand. "Do not say what you are going to. I would not have the strength to deny you if you did. Let me do this for you."

"Stop."

We both jerked as a rich voice rumbled through the room. At first, wildly maybe, I thought that it was Wei, but I turned and saw Vlad Tepes, father of all vampires, standing at the edge of the bed.

"Get out of here," Zane snapped. I was surprised to hear someone take that tone with Vlad. I fully expected the master vampire to get angry, but instead he smiled. He looked almost proud.

"You are not the only one who needs to make amends, my son." Vlad glanced at me with dark eyes, and then bowed. "I am an imperfect man, Lorena Quinn, and I let my desires outdo me."

I didn't know what to say to that. It was an apology, sure, but I wasn't really ready to forgive him. "What are you doing here?"

Vlad picked up another IV, and stuck it in his arm. "I will not lose two sons today."

I was about to say something, I don't know what, but I felt like arguing with him. I didn't want Vlad's blood in Wei's veins. But the moment the blood went from tube to flesh Wei's whole body jerked and suddenly I didn't care if a load of serial killers were hooked up to Wei, so long as he lived.

I rushed to Wei's side and took his hand in mine. His fingers weren't as gnarled as they had been. They were still cool beneath my touch, but fleshy. His eyes went from hazy to clear, his lips softened.

"Lorena?"

It was the first word out of his mouth, and I shivered to hear it.

"I'm here."

He didn't breathe out a sigh of relief, vampires don't need to breathe, but he seemed to sag against the metal just the same. "I knew you'd come for me."

"Because I love you?" I asked.

His not quite healed lips curled into a smile. "No, because you are stubborn."

I laughed, and I kissed him, and then I laughed again. Everything was going to be just fine.

THE FINAL CHAPTER

It took my five years to learn to create my pocket dimension, and it was worth every moment.

Things moved fast and then slow when we finally left the temple behind us. My father officially moved into his mother's house, and I moved out of it, back into the mansion. Marquessa Green, executor of the estate released the funds back to me, and I gave them to my dad. He used them to go to school, and eventually he became a math teacher. It suits him, and he is finally happy with himself, and come to terms with his mother's life and death.

Jenny and Reikah got married. They day they made it legal the pair of them were at the courthouse. I held Jenny's hand as she signed the papers. Reikah wore the prettiest sari that I have ever seen, and Jenny put a golden ring on her finger with a single stone in it. It was a beautiful day.

Alan and Dmitri didn't get married. They traveled the world together with Peter to look after them. I have received letters and gifts from Russia, Wales, France, and Germany. Someone introduced Dmitri to the iPhone and now I get at least once picture of them a day...or rather...night. They are the cutest couple and their love is pathetically cute.

Genevieve left Vlad. I'm not entirely sure what did it, but she left him. I was surprised that Yasmina went with her. I wish I had gotten a chance to understand them a little better, but I am happy for them both. I think Genevieve has a boyfriend, but she's being very tight lipped about it. Yasmina works at a bar in Richmond.

Vlad and his remaining wife and daughters, who seem happy enough together, went back to Vlad's castle. I think they brood there. I still haven't forgiven him for locking me up and trying to force the prophecy.

My pocket dimension is perfect, at least as far as I am concerned.

It's a main street in the middle of a small town with seven buildings. One shop is a book store, one a coffee shop, one a comic and gaming store, a pizza parlor, one is an apartment with four bedrooms, one is a witch's supply shop, I work there, and one is a carpenter's workshop. Guess who works there?

The pocket dimension is filled with the ghosts of people who have nowhere to go and don't want to move on. They know my name, I know them, and we live together in a town I feel like I've always belonged in. I've named the pseudo-town Paradise, because that's what it is for me.

The scent of herbs and crystals fills my nose as I lock up my shop. Business today was good. Ghosts from all over the world come to visit me. Sometimes they bring herbs, tokens, or trinkets from wherever they come from and trade them for something else. I've learned that ghosts like to have things as much as they did while they were alive.

A dark hand slides over my cheek and I turn to accept the kiss that I know is coming. Zane smells like wine and pizza sauce and his lips are gentle. There is a child sitting on his hip. The child looks like us. My hazel eyes stare at me out of a round, softly brown face. His lips are already smirking as he reaches out for me.

"Mommy!" he cries happily. I take him in my arms and give him a hug. "Hello, Michael," I say kissing his forehead. "What did you do today?"

I am regaled with a babbling story about the pizza place and the ducks who came to visit. There very well may have been ducks. My son has the same way with animals that my half-sister had.

Zane's arm wraps around my back and we both listen to Michael talk as we walk next door to the carpenter's shop.

Wei works without a shirt on and when I approach his dark eyes sparkle with amusement. There is a little girl, a year older than the boy, sitting on a table, her legs swing as she sips from a coffee cup.

"She's too young for coffee," I chide lightly. She's too young for a lot of things. I haven't told her about the prophecy yet. I think telling a four-year-old that she's going to bring magic back into the world is a lot to set on her shoulders.

Wei shrugs his shoulders. He's never been able to deny Fai anything. It's both annoying and sweet. "She likes it."

I roll my eyes, and he comes over to kiss me too. He smells like wood and warmth. I like it.

I won't say that being in love with two men is easy. It's not. There is a lot of balance and energy, but at the end of the day, when I curl up in their arms, I know that it's worth it.

"Hi, Mommy," Fai says hopping off the bench. She does not come running to me, or reach out the way Michael does. Fai has always been more independent. Her dark hair, so like Wei's, sweeps nearly the length of her back as she looks up at me with her dark eyes.

"I made you something," she tells me.

"Oh?" I say, pleasure already curling my lips. "What is it?"

She reaches beneath the table that she sat on, and pulls out what looks to be an egg, though it's large enough to be an ostrich's . I blink and take it. It's heavy, and carved of a wood so dark it's almost black. The surface shines with light, but not a light that exists in the shop. A moment later I realize the light is coming from inside the egg.

"It's beautiful," I say. "How did you do that?"

She gives me a look. "I made it." She says it like it explains absolutely everything. "It'll bring magic to the world."

Wei, Zane, and I all go very, very still.

"What?" I say after a moment of tense silence.

Fai gives me a smile. "It's what dragons do, Mommy."

***

Dear Reader,

Thank you so much for reading all the way to the end.

If you enjoyed the final book then it then it would mean so much to me if you could leave **a review on Amazon.** Even just a sentence would be amazing!

If you want to see more of my work, just head over to my author page (link below)

SAMANTHA SNOW AMAZON PAGE

Thanks for reading and making "house of vampires" a bestselling series on Amazon.com!

See you in the next book

Samantha x x

Get Yourself a FREE Bestselling Paranormal Romance Book!

Join the "**Simply Shifters**" Mailing list today and gain access to an exclusive **FREE** classic Paranormal Shifter Romance book by one of our bestselling authors along with many others more to come. You will also be kept up to date on the best book deals in the future on the hottest new Paranormal Romances. We are the HOME of Paranormal Romance after all!

* Get FREE Shifter Romance Books For Your Kindle & Other Cool giveaways

* Discover Exclusive Deals & Discounts Before Anyone Else!

* Be The FIRST To Know about Hot New Releases From Your Favorite Authors

Click The Link Below To Access Get All This Now!

SimplyShifters.com

Already subscribed?
OK, *Turn The Page!*

ALSO BY SIMPLY SHIFTERS....

SIMPLY VAMPIRES
A TEN BOOK VAMPIRE ROMANCE COLLECTION

99c or FREE to read with Kindle Unlimited

This unique 10 book package features some of the best selling authors from the world of Paranormal Romance. The perfect blend of love, sex and adventure involving curvy, cute heroines and their handsome vampire lovers.

Book 1 - JJ Jones – The White Vampire
Book 2 – Samantha Snow – A Lighter Shade Of Pale
Book 3 - Amira Rain – Melted By The Vampire
Book 4 - Serena Rose – Prince Lucien
Book 5 – Ellie Valentina – Red Solstice
Book 6 - Bonnie Burrows – The Vampire's Shared Bride
Book 7 - Jade White – Never Have A Vampires Baby
Book 8 - Angela Foxxe – A Billion Secrets
Book 9 - Samantha Snow - Spawn Of The Vampire
Book 10 - Jasmine White – Bitten By The Bad Boy

TAP HERE TO DOWNLOAD THIS NOW!

Printed in Great Britain
by Amazon